The Divine Brexit Comedy

A political satire, based on
The Divine Comedy by Dante Alighieri

S.C. Burrows

To my husband and my cousin, without whom this book
would not have been written.

"Now preachers go with feeble jokes and gags
and, just so long as they can raise a laugh,
their hoods puff up. They ask for nothing more.
A devil bird, though, nestles in their cowls.
Were folk to see this, they would see (they must!)
what sort of pardons these are they so trust.
And so such idiocy grows on earth
That all, without good evidence or proof,
Chase after every promise they hear made."

The Divine Comedy by Dante Alighieri, 1321
(Kirkpatrick translation)

CONTENTS

Acknowledgments   i

Preface   ii

1   Unexpected Changes   1

2   Entering Hell   11

3   Across the Styx   22

4   Delving the Ditches of Deception   41

5   The Darkest Depths   74

Diagram of Dante's Hell   88

ACKNOWLEDGMENTS

This book is based on Dante Alighieri's original work.
My appreciation of the Italian original was greatly
enhanced by two translations into English:
- Dante 'The Divine Comedy', translated by Robin
  Kirkpatrick, Penguin Classics, 2012
- 'The Inferno of Dante': a new verse translation by
  Robert Pinsky, bilingual edition, Farrar, Straus and
  Giroux, 1994.

The map of Dante's Hell at the end of the book is
reprinted from Lapham's Quarterly, "Crime and
Punishment," Vol. 2, No. 2 (Spring 2009),
https://www.laphamsquarterly.org/.

PREFACE

2021 was the 7th centenary of Dante Alighieri's 'The Divine Comedy'. The first part of that three-part epic is 'Inferno' (Italian for 'Hell'). In it, Dante is guided down through nine circles of Hell to Satan. In each circle he witnesses the eternal punishment meted out to historical characters, guilty of the principal human vices. Prompted by the centenary celebrations to read Dante, I was immediately struck by how relevant it was to Brexit politics – 700 years later. I was inspired to write this short, satirical rendition.

Since most readers will not be familiar with Dante's 'Inferno', let me explain how this 'Divine Brexit Comedy' works. It follows strictly the structure and scenes of Dante's 'Inferno', but with contemporary characters. Each Circle of Hell deals with the specific human vices Dante described and were also clearly demonstrated during the Brexit process.

You will find a schematic 'map' of Dante's 'Inferno' at the back of the book.

1 UNEXPECTED CHANGES

[Canto 1 & 2] I consider I have held up pretty well over the years – centuries, even. Perhaps not quite as vigorous and overwhelming as in my heyday, but still a force to be reckoned with. I am not one to get nervous, even alone in a foreign city in the dead of night, or in a wild wood, such as this, among looming, ancient trees that block the sun for much of the day. Alert: yes. On my guard: sometimes. Nervous: never. Not in my vocabulary. I can defend myself pretty well against most dangers. But that day felt strange. I found myself searching through a wood I thought I knew well, impelled down a path I had never walked before. Everything around me felt alien and sinister, the way it does in a bad dream. Before I knew it, I was lost. My name? Britannia. Did I not mention?

Soon, I was entangled in a thick mass of briars of red tape. Here and there, they were crushed by the recently fallen boughs of suffering businesses, but new growth was rapid. The thorns were vicious, tenacious barbs of new forms and bureaucratic demands that hooked fast in my robes and the exposed flesh on my arms. My ankles were snared by sharp-edged tendrils of new regulations. My skin tore as I lunged forward with my shield and slashed away the undergrowth with my short sword. When I looked back, my own trail seemed to have closed behind me. I had no choice but to keep moving onward.

Just a couple of years ago, this wood stretched down to an inlet from the sea. In the last hundred metres, the light through the trees brightened, reflecting off the dancing water. As you emerged on to the shore, the breeze would caress your face, scudding off rippled wavelets. Boats buzzed chaotically back and forth. The inlet was narrow enough to see streams of commercial traffic to and from the wharves and buildings stretched along the far shore and deep enough to teem with fish. But on this day, when I reached the beach, I could hardly believe my eyes. The water was almost still. Only two boats chugged sluggishly in the middle, loaded to the gunwales.

Scattered on the beach at my feet, where once we played and bathed, lay bodies of mackerel, herring, big langoustine, and scallops; some dried out, some stinking as they rotted. A couple of gulls jabbed at the remains. I gritted my teeth: what unnecessary destruction!

On my right, the inlet had flooded up into the wood, creating a wasteland of bare, water-logged trunks. Some had lost branches. Several whole trunks had succumbed and toppled into the black stagnant water. Nothing moved. My insides hollowed. I wandered closer.

"I can't take much more," said a voice. Close by.

"You think you've got problems, mate," came another voice, lower in pitch.

I turned my head, left, right, concentrating. But there was no-one there. Only the dying trees.

"Yes, I do. I lost a quarter of my sales overnight with all the new taxes on internet sales to European consumers. See that branch down there. That was mine."

"See that one over there," came the second voice again. "Lost all her leaves overnight. And they won't be returning next season. She's a goner. Used to bear so much fruit. Won't be much longer before she keels over."

"Yes, well, I have to concentrate on my own survival in this mess."

"What really gets me is the lies. I thought it would be a good thing. But global supply chain problems, my arse. I've got orders to my eyeballs, but I can't get the drivers. Trucks standing unused."

"But you can train up new ones," said the first voice. "Me, I have to shift all my planned new investment to Europe, if I want to keep the customers."

"Train up new ones! It takes time. There's a massive national shortage. I am competing with all the others. Plus, I really need drivers with experience. It's just one hurdle after another. I have been here for three generations, but I'm not sure how much longer I can survive. It breaks my heart to think it'll all go under on my watch."

Now I was the one who could take it no more. But this was not the moment for self-pity. I pivoted away from the struggling and dying and walked back towards those trees that were still thriving.

Ahead, I spotted a new plantation, at a safe distance from the shore. Young, green trees thrusting upwards. My mood brightened for an instant. But I knew those trees would take a long time to reach maturity and productivity. What's more, the new plantation was a good deal smaller than the graveyard of trees behind me. I sighed and trudged along the beach, past the new plantation, and stepped into the wood again.

I seemed to be walking downhill and into a narrowing ravine. Banks of rock, at first pale, closed in. The walls swelled higher, steeper and darker. There were no birds; in fact, no sounds at all. The place felt cold and damp, dripping. Huge clumps of nettles assaulted my feet and ankles. Spider's webs spanned across the path. I stumbled over lumps of fallen rock, glanced up to check for imminent danger of more ... and stumbled again. With my face lowered, I spotted a sizeable sink-hole in front of me, obscured by thick ferns and more nettles. Big enough to swallow me! Scanning wider, I saw more: large sink-holes. Was this where once there had been thriving markets for manufactured goods and services? Struggling with the undergrowth, I slashed a safe path around them.

But then the smell started. At first, quite faint, soon overwhelming, cloying at the back of my throat. This was no dead mouse. Reeling, I almost trod on the first of the corpses. Heaving with maggots, eyes pecked out, and chunks of meat and limbs torn off. Pigs. Not wild boar. Farm pigs, grown for meat. Slaughtered and dumped here in grotesque piles. I pulled my cloak over my mouth, repelling dizziness, and pushed forward and beyond. It took me a full ten minutes to negotiate that killing field. My eyes blurred. But now there was just enough of a strip ahead, winding through the undergrowth, to keep me moving as the darkness closed in.

As I walked, I worried. Of course, I have been through similar periods, when people under my mantle took decisions in an instant, despite major long-term consequences. It is always uncomfortable for me. But it is part of the job.

Then the pain started. What was happening? Why was I even still walking? It felt as though fibres in my limbs were stretching beyond endurance, tearing and ripping; as if I were on the rack, being pulled apart. And in my gut, an invisible hand twisted and squeezed.

I told myself it is like sport. You know, 'No Gain without Pain'. I just needed to distract myself a while. I thought of other momentous periods of turmoil that strengthened me in the end.

There were many over the centuries, since the Romans. But first up today popped 24 March 1603, when James IV of Scotland ascended to the throne of England and Wales as well, as James I. That is how it could be. Uniting nations could make me stronger. Next, there were the Acts of Union 1801, creating the United Kingdom of Great Britain and Ireland. Yes, well, let's not go there. I have made many awful mistakes in the past, caused millions of people a great deal of anguish. Hundreds of thousands have died and the corpses haunt me. Shame eats at me when I think of them. But guilt serves no-one, unless used as a spur to improve. I have learned a lot about oppression, freedom, justice and respect. Focus on that, I told myself.

Despite my mental efforts, the pain began to overwhelm me. I stopped to check for blood from an unfelt wound. All was sound. But I was fading, the loss of power persisted. I was becoming lesser. I began to hallucinate.

Neighbour nations - ones I love deeply and others I don't particularly like, but we rub along as part of a larger family - stood with their arms around each other, legs braced, as the earth shook and tilted from level to a steep slope with them at the top. I felt myself sliding backwards, down, away from them. Several held one arm stretched out towards me and pleaded "Reach, stretch. Don't leave us!" But my hand would not lift. I tried, I tried, but it just wouldn't lift. As I slid backwards, slowly, but unstoppable, I knew there was a cliff edge behind me.

I shook the nightmare from my head. A heavy, damp cloak of Fear settled on me. Me of all people.

At dawn, a warm light spread over a peaked mountain at the head of this menacing gorge and beckoned me forward. The rocky summit and broad, fertile shoulders above the tree-line were bathed in yellow glow. The fear and searing pain retreated back down the ravine. I responded with renewed energy. Only hunger and tiredness slowed my pace a little.

As I reached the lower slopes, out of nowhere, a Leopard stood in front of me. Lithe and alert, it stared me down. I froze. Lowering my gaze, I cowered downwards in mock deference. I started to back away. The Leopard stared. I backed a few paces further. She twitched her tail and then turned her gaze over her shoulder towards the summit. Decision made, she pivoted and bounded effortlessly upwards. At that moment, a ray of sunlight pierced through the leaves and shone on her dappled coat. Hope surged through me and I followed her quietly. But she soon sprang away into the undergrowth. I pressed on, heartened.

Next, a huge Lion leapt from the bushes some way up the path and charged towards me, shaking his thick mane and roaring so loud the air trembled. I held my shield in such a way that the sun would reflect off it and dazzle him. But I also prepared to roll into the thickest brambles and cover myself like a Roman soldier. His roar stopped as suddenly as it had started. I peered around my shield. A painfully thin she-wolf was stalking towards me in the Lion's place. She looked as though she held the cravings of all the poor and hungry of this world inside her. I shuddered. Every bubble of Hope inside me burst. I felt so heavy I could hardly move, though I knew I should retreat fast, back to where there was no sun and my nightmares lurked, ready to consume me.

At that moment, the figure of a man appeared in the trees just to the right of the path. Was he human? It seemed ephemeral. An hallucination? Or, worse, a spectre? Either way, I had to know. I called for his help, whether alive or dead. He replied:

"I am no longer alive, though once I was. Born under Julius Caesar, I was a poet. My parents were Mantuans from Lombardy. But why do you retreat back to the misery down there? Why not climb this mountain?"

The She-Wolf had stopped, her eyes glowed yellow with a craving and evil I can hardly describe. Her dull, grey coat hung from the points of her hips and her ribs showed clearly in her hollow flanks. Head level with her spine, drool dripped from her panting mouth.

'Virgil?' I asked. "Can it be you? Your work inspired me so much. You provide the model for civic life that I have strived towards. But yesterday I took a path I had never seen before and have no idea where I am now. Help me, please, to deal with this ghastly creature."

"Yes, you can better take a different route around her.

She lets nothing pass."

Still she stood, panting and slathering. But she made no move towards me as Virgil spoke, so I took the opportunity to ask again what this strange place was and the menacing creatures.

"You have been struggling through post-Brexit Britain. This, around us now, is the Forest of Truth and Untruth, of Fact and Alternative Fact, of Information and Misinformation. There are many, many species here." He nodded his head towards the dark forest behind me. Then raising his arm upwards to indicate the mountain, still bathed in light, he continued. "This is the Mountain of Perfect Cooperation between the nations of Europe. Here, their different strengths and talents, born of their diverse origins and history, are embraced and channelled to carry all forward, compensating for the shortcomings that hold each one back from reaching its potential. Together they are stronger towards the world beyond their collective borders."

"It's an enticing vision," I said. "But how do these vicious animals come in to the picture?"

"Ah," said Virgil. "Do you not recognize them and see them for what they are?"

I frowned and shook my head.

"I seem to be blind on that one, kind sir", I said.

"Each one is a menace on the path to the summit of this mountain. The first, the Leopard, is Bureaucracy. The second, the Lion, is Corruption. They are not everywhere, but where they roam, they are dangerous enemies and killers too. And this one here…." he pointed at the She-Wolf. She snarled. I could not help myself from stepping back, which she spotted and advanced towards me again. I stood my ground and raised my shield. It would not do to look cowardly in front of Virgil. The Wolf halted.

"This one, she is the Wolf of Intercultural Miscommunication and Historical Baggage", said Virgil.

"An ugly name." I ventured.

"An ugly name for an ugly and insidious beast. The most malign and vicious of them all. She spreads suspicion wherever she treads. Left untreated, it festers into fear and loathing of the deepest kind. She herself was born of Envy and in her life has mothered so many litters of offspring, fathered by many beasts, that she is sucked dry. Feeding her makes her hungrier. The only Hound that can vanquish her and send her back to Hell, from where she came, will be fed by Wisdom, Goodness and Love."

"But isn't there a whole chain of Mountains?" I asked. "Each with its peak in the sun. Some may be a little higher than others, but all have fertile ground, a beautiful view and a dominant position. And aren't they all linked together anyway? What's so special about this one? Is it in some way better than the others, apart from the fact that it's the closest?"

Virgil sighed and smiled slightly. "I cannot answer those questions."

He clearly was not going to say more nor leave. He simply stood. So I changed tack:

"Well, first things first, could I ask you to help me get around this creature and find my way back to where I came from?"

"Britannia, you cannot go back. The only way out now is through. Follow me away from here on a roundabout route through an eternal place. You will hear desperate souls crying out for relief from their suffering and those stuck in fire, who hoped that one day they would ascend to the promised 'sunlit uplands' you see above you there. You must descend, before you can rise again. That is your duty. Should you wish to mount there too, you will need another guide later. But I can take you through the first part so that you may know the way and the why."

That seemed unnecessarily enigmatic. But I sensed he was not going to say more at this point and I needed him. So, I thanked him profusely and edged my way cautiously round to where he stood. He turned away from the Wolf. I followed in silence, wrapped in my thoughts. I forced myself not to look back. It was getting dark again – the time most creatures prepare to sleep. But I felt I was girding up for a major struggle. Quite why, I could not say.

[Canto 3] At the end of a long, quiet wooded road, we came to a door. Arched above it ran a sign, which exclaimed: "Through me you enter the City of Woe; through me you go to eternal pain; through me you join the lost people. Abandon all hope, Ye who enter here". Intimidating, even for me. I looked at Virgil, quizzically.

"Here you must leave all fear and cowardice," he announced. "From this point on we will meet those who have lost the good that comes from using your intellect."

Try as I might, my face must have betrayed some surprise and doubt at what we might be about to witness. Virgil took my hand and smiled and led me forward. Never one to back down when courage is needed - though I prefer to be well-prepared - I set my stride boldly alongside his.

Then I began to hear the sighs and moans in the dark. As we advanced, the noise crescendoed into sobs and gut-wrenching groans. Louder still came howls of rage, smacking of hands, and slapping flesh. The noises whirled around me, like a sandstorm. My head spun. I could contain myself no longer.

"Who are these people?"

"They are those who lived for themselves alone with no sense of civic rights or responsibilities. They did no active wrong, so Hell will not take them. But they did not participate either. So they cannot pass to the 'sunlit uplands'. They chose neither side in the Great Debate. They are apathetic; the first to be hanging here in Limbo, lamenting that this is where they will stay for ever."

He moved on and I stayed close to him. I tried not to look at the ribbons of wretched people around us and wondered: didn't Aristotle have something to say about Apathy?

Shortly a river came in sight. It was no Nile, but wide and deep enough to need a boat to cross. As we approached the shore, the crowd thickened.

"Here are those who chose not to vote and now regret it," explained Virgil.

"Vote? Which vote?"

"Ah, Britannia! Are you so slow? Do not leave your intellect behind here with them," he laughed and gestured towards the multitudes around us. I can't say I found it funny. "Have you not yet understood? This is the River of the Brexit Referendum."

My stomach sank; my jaw too. I almost dropped my shield. I froze. What was happening here? What was I about to witness? Worse, what would be asked of me? 'Abandon all hope, Ye who enter here'. The words bounced behind my eyes.

Seeing my shock, Virgil gently took my hand again and led me to the shore, where a boat approached. At the helm was another vile, but humanoid, creature with red eyes. Despite the creature's protests, Virgil managed to get us both aboard and we arrived safely on the other side, unaccompanied by the hordes we had left behind.

Exhausted, physically and mentally, I wrapped myself in my cloak and fell deep asleep on the bare ground, beyond dreams.

2 ENTERING HELL

[Canto 4] I was woken by thunder rolling, very close. It took me a while to come round. Images of the previous days' events flashed in my head. I heaved myself up and looked around. The patch of ground, where I had slept, fell away just a few metres from me. Good thing I stopped where I did last night. I stepped cautiously towards the edge to assess the size of this abyss. Swirling cloud obscured the view, but I saw enough to gauge that it was a vast, funnel-shaped crater. The depths were a black hole of absolute darkness, sucking energy in to the core. I jumped back. Virgil stood next to me, his face pale.

"Let us descend," he said solemnly. "I will go first. You follow close behind me."

His face was so full of dread, I had to ask: "How can I follow if you are so afraid? What is this place? And what will we encounter?"

"It is the agony of those down there that affects me. Pity, not fear," he replied. "I think you already know that you are here to witness and understand this place and confront the beasts that writhe in its depths. Thereafter you will travel on through Purgatory in order to attain those sunlit uplands you so admired earlier. Only in this way can you and your people heal and recover the values you embody, your strength and dignity. It is your duty.

"We will go down through nine levels. As we go, much will be revealed to feed your learning for recovery. You will see lost souls from throughout history but meet only with those that touch your story. Our journey will get much worse, before it can get better. But there is no other path to redemption."

He set off in slow, steady paces. I took some time to absorb what he had said and prepare myself mentally. But, strangely, a part of me had indeed already begun to know that only I could heal the pain I had been suffering earlier. Only I could cure myself. I strode forward purposefully to catch up with Virgil.

Over the lip of the abyss, the light faded immediately. I still had no idea how long this journey would be and what shape it would take. 'Nine levels' did not tell me much. I know now that we had entered the **First Circle**. At first, I thought it was the wind, but soon I realized that what I heard were sighs, so many the air trembled. They sounded weary beyond limits, but not in pain. How many were there? Multitudes?

Virgil paused and turned. "Before you ask, these have never sinned. And some did merit-worthy acts. But that is not enough. They will remain here in Limbo for ever."

Virgil led me on through the throngs of sighing spirits, so crowded I would not have been able to see the way, even had there been sufficient light. My heart went out to these poor souls. They had not deliberately harmed others. Did they merit being stuck in this No-Man's Land?

Ahead, I saw the glow of a fire, hovering above a denser patch of shadow. As we approached, five of the Ancient Greek and Roman philosophers and poets appeared and welcomed us forward to the dome of light. It rose above a massive fort: their Fort of Common Peace among City States. There they resided in a calm, green haven, at peace, but confined to discussing amongst themselves. They were all there, too many to list here. As we arrived, I thought I spotted Aristotle, sitting in intense concentration in a sunny spot with a scroll and quill. I overcame my awe sufficiently to exchange a few words with Ovid and Socrates, before Virgil took my elbow and led me back out into the trembling dark. Later, he explained. The fort sheltered the great intellects from ancient times, whose work laid the foundations of many of the aspirations, principles and values at the heart of contemporary European civic culture. They shaped the concepts for Good Living in the time of common peace between the Greek city states. But since they lived before structured international cooperation between sovereign nation states, before the League of Nations, before the Universal Declaration of Human Rights, before the European Union, they could not advance further. They would have to be content to linger in their peaceful haven and Virgil himself would rejoin them, when our journey ends.

[*Canto 5*] Shocked by the fate of all these revered philosophers and poets, I followed Virgil in silence. What could I say? Was Lady Justice asleep? We moved on down to the **Second Circle.** Here the real misery began. Here stood the judge of guilt, towering over all those who approached. Each arrival was pierced to a halt by his blue eyes. He breathed in deep and drew himself up to his full height, as if preparing to blow out the candles on a birthday cake appropriate to his age, and asked for their story. His neatly combed, silvered head made a small circling motion while they spoke, as if he were trying to wind them up to finish faster. I watched and wondered if he really listened or had already used his acute senses, refined over years of experience, to decide in an instant what special place in Hell awaited each comer. Even before they finished, he raised his arms, palms turned outward, and paused. And then he pronounced each one's fate in smooth, polished tones, flavoured with a French accent, a hint of impatience and a whiff of fish: "You to Circle Four. You to Circle Six. *Tout de suite.*"

As Virgil tried to take us, unnoticed, by a side path, his laser-sharp eyes swung and pinned our feet to the bare ground. "Be careful who you trust and don't be fooled," he said. Seconds ticked. Then, calmly, he turned his gaze away and we could pass on.

The weeping and sorrowful laments began in earnest. As the winds of Hell picked up, so did the squalls of keening cries and shouts of sharp pain. Buffeted by the swirling storms of uncontrolled passions, flung violently in all directions, I saw them, the lustful Members of the European Parliament. Now they felt the consequences of their exuberant partying and unrestrained shagging of every colleague or intern who took their fancy. Sent to Brussels to do a serious job, they had allowed themselves to be overwhelmed by their large expense accounts in the city of 'bon humeur' and indulged their carnal appetites without a second thought. Here they would rot, bruised and aching from the eternal buffeting of the winds that punished their vice. Without pity, as far as I was concerned.

[Canto 6] As we descended further, the wind faded and the rain began. At first just a smattering of heavy, ice-cold drops. I pulled my cloak tighter over my head and round my body. But as we entered the **Third Circle**, it intensified, lashing down in torrents, mixed with sleety snow and squalls of hailstones the size of golf balls. Shoulders hunched, I set my face downwards, away from the bitingly cold deluge and concentrated on my foothold in the slippery, stinking black mud. The smell turned my stomach. I breathed as shallow as I could. I began to suspect that with each layer of descent into this funnel-shaped crater, the intensity of suffering and unpleasantness would increase.

A cacophony of blood-curdling howls just in front stopped my heart and steps. There stood Cerberus, the three-headed hound. His eyes were vermillion red, his fur greasy black, pulled taut over his meat-filled belly. Around him in the quagmire lay fleshy, naked bodies, their folds of fat glowed pale blue-grey, daubed with mud. As he growled and howled, his talon-like claws flayed their skin and carved their flesh into bite-size pieces. They squirmed. Were all those howls from one of his foul mouths? Definitely not.

"In case you haven't guessed yet, this is where the Gluttons languish," whispered Virgil.

Cerberus spotted us. All three heads turned our way. They snarled, lips curled back, and all three slathering muzzles opened wide to show us the length of his fangs. I was shaking with cold and, I have to admit again, some trepidation.

"Prepare to run", hissed Virgil through his teeth, without moving his lips or head. Then, quick as a flash, he bent and picked up handfuls of the vile black mud. He flung them hard into each of the waiting throats. Thinking he had received a snack, Cerberus' jaws closed and he fell silent for a moment, like any farmyard cur. We rushed past, sliding and squelching. It only took a moment for the evil hound to realise he had been tricked, but it was long enough for us. His angry barks pursued us. I wished I were deaf.

Once we were at a safe distance, I started to look around again through the curtains of freezing rain. Among all the Rubenesque figures floundering in the mud, I noticed one woman. She cowered against a rock; her whole body caved inward. She was as naked as the rest, but thin. Her skin was beginning to sag. Neatly-cut, grey hair was plastered wet to her skull, which made her beak-like nose more prominent. She stared at the ground. Her lips moved quietly and she picked at her hands and finger nails obsessively. I caught Virgil's elbow.

"But what about her?" I asked. "She doesn't look like a glutton."

"Ah. We can speak to her if you wish." He ushered me towards her.

As we neared, I could hear her words.

"Just the cherry. That's all. I can only eat the cherries", she repeated, as if on a loop. Her head twitched slightly.

"Madam", murmured Virgil. She stood, surprisingly tall, but stooped.

"Just the cherries. That's all", she pleaded and held her torn hands out towards me. "I can't eat the cake. It's my digestion, you see. Just the cherries on top." She pointed to something behind me. I glanced back. There was nothing but rain and black mud. She lifted her large grey eyes to mine and her sad gaze went vacant, before she collapsed back down into the mud in a bony heap. That is when I noticed the small knife shaft protruding from beside her left shoulder blade.

Distressed by surprising pangs of pity, I turned and stepped away. Virgil caught up with me.

"Who was she, Virgil? Why is she here?"

"You don't recognize her?" he asked. "She had to lead, after the River was crossed. Pressured from all sides by her own team, her own political party, she tried to pick only the cherries from the tops of the cakes and leave the bulk. It's a special form of gluttony. Their guilt became hers. Leave the European Union, leave the Single Market, leave the Customs Union, leave the European Court of Justice … but still participate in just a few key European Union programmes without any wider obligations. You cannot say you want to leave the club and pay no dues, but keep attending the special events and help make the rules. She didn't have the vision or skills to find a workable way through. She sank beneath the weight of impossible demands. In the final act, someone from her own party stabbed her in the back. If you complete your mission successfully, she may yet be redeemed."

He closed his mouth, lifted his chin and strode off. I hurried behind, slipping and sliding.

A few paces further, I spotted another middle-aged woman. At least, I thought she was a woman: big-boned and strong with a firm square jaw, which could also have been a man's. She lurched towards us. "The Divided City will fall. There will be violence. I didn't see; I didn't see," she wailed in a strong Belfast accent. "He betrayed me. They all betrayed me."

"Madam," I ventured. "Surely you would not be in this vile place, if you bore no fault at all yourself. Tell me more."

"We were doing well," she insisted passionately. "Trade was flowing better than ever, both to the south and to the mainland. You can never truly trust a Papist, of course, but we don't mind accepting their money. We are a creative lot. And we work hard. I had led us to a good place."

She nodded in the direction of the wretched woman we had just passed and continued: "When the Thin One over there called an election at the wrong moment for her, stupid woman, we struck gold. We got real power. We had ten seats in Westminster. Without us, the government's majority was not secure. Our votes were decisive. We even struck a special deal with the London government. Tiny, we may be, but we were punching way above our weight. We held sway. The Thin One, she tried to dilute the Brexit with her 'backstop'. Well, I could see what was coming. Before you know it, there'd be a United Ireland. We'd be cut adrift and left to hold our own with the Papists. No, no, not for us, thank you. We'd be out-numbered from the start. And that lot breed like rabbits."

"Wait, wait," I said. "Cut adrift from what, Madam?"

"From you," she scoffed. "From you, Britannia!" and poked her finger at my face. I stepped back. Now I knew. But there was no stopping her.

"And after we'd brought the Thin One down, I went to meet him, the Big Blond. I had my delegation with me. We knew we held the strings. He knew we held the strings. We all huffed and puffed a bit. You know how it goes. Then, he promised me to my face, mind, to my face, and in front of the cameras, that if we agreed to his 'oven-ready deal', we could keep our unfettered traffic with those down South as well as with our brothers and sisters on the mainland. No borders anywhere. Over his dead body would there be a border of any sort in the Irish Sea. He promised. But look now. "

"You mean you sought to have your cake and eat it too?" asked Virgil quietly. Perhaps he meant it to be an aside.

"Oooooh," she wailed. "He lied, that Big Blond. He lied to my face. And now the Divided City is more divided than it has been in years. And which of us rots here in this vile, stinking place? Not him! Oh woe!" she sobbed and sank down on her knees in the black mud.

What could I say? 'How stupid can you get?' That wouldn't really help her, would it? Or me. But greed for power can be a costly thing. It was not she alone who paid the price of her mistakes. 'May your hubris eat you from the inside out.' But I kept quiet.

As I looked at her, sobbing in the filth, it began again: the pain I had felt back in the forest at the start. The stretching, stretching of my limbs beyond endurance, as if I were strapped to the rack. Something, something must give and I ..... would be torn apart. I shook my head and turned away abruptly, rubbing my arms beneath my cloak.

This journey was proving harder than I had imagined. But did I have a choice? Must I really wait until the end before defending myself? As I brooded, we rounded the curve and the path came to the brow of a new dip down to the **Fourth Circle.**

[Canto 7] The path was blocked by a lupine horror: Plutus. Jaws foaming, he snarled and muttered gibberish. Virgil urged me not to hesitate and he himself advanced.

"Silence, cursed wolf! Let your rage eat you from the inside out. We are on a special mission and WE SHALL PASS!" he shouted.

The beast collapsed inward, like wind-filled sails at the moment the mast snaps. I could not believe it was so easy. I had picked the right guide. We passed on, hugging the rock wall.

Two factions of people, even more numerous than we had yet seen in the previous Circles, rolled enormous boulders around the perimeter wall towards each other from opposing sides of this vast crater. They shoved and heaved with all their weight, legs braced, leaning in from shoulder or chest to hip. Between their breathless efforts, they screamed abuse at each other.

"You wasters! Profligates!" screamed the one faction. "Why do you throw so much away? You're squandering our hard-earned tax money. Out of control budgets! And why should we pay for fat-cat salaries of Brussels bureaucrats, who have no idea of the real world. We can better use it on our NHS. We must take back control. You only think in millions and billions. You're being ripped off in every contract. It's a scandal. Take back control! Take back control!"

"You misers! You hoarders!" shouted the other faction. "Why are you so mean? Don't you get it? The gains we all stand to make are worth the investment. Together we are rich. We can afford to support our poorest regions. We must help our farmers, wherever they are. Spend, we say. In the end, we'll benefit anyway. You'll see. And no more can we abandon those knocking on our doors, fleeing from terror and starvation outside our borders. You can't leave people to die. It's inhumane. We can afford to help them for now. And it will cost us more in the end, if we don't. Spend! Spend!"

I saw words emblazoned on the boulders: 'Common Agriculture Policy', 'Red Tape', 'Brussels Fat Cats' on the boulders of the first faction. 'Europol', 'Regional Subsidies', 'Data Exchange', 'Erasmus' were daubed on the boulders of the second faction.

Eventually their stones clashed. At this point, they wheeled round, shrieking their chants, and heaved their boulders back along the half circle, until they clashed again at the diametric points. And thus it went on, condemned never to understand each other or find a balance between the two extremes.

I watched in awe. Sisyphus had nothing on this. This is how dogma drives human squabbles to extremes where none can benefit and all beauty, invention and creativity is lost. Dogma is the circus master and money his whip to drive humans so easily into tornadoes of hatred, round and round, blowing Mutual Respect out of the window.

"Hmmm. You're right", said Virgil, before I had said anything. I turned, my eyes deliberately wide, eyebrows raised and mouth half open. He had read my mind – and not for the first time.

"Excuse me," I said. "I haven't spoken yet."

He laughed. "Excuse me, dear Britannia. I see that you are beginning to see. They are all so greatly hurt by their own obstinacy and fixation on money, but from opposite sides. Let us move on, down to greater pain".

Those last words snuffed out the first flicker of levity I had felt since this journey began. It could not end well. But, as before, I followed Virgil's lead.

We cut across the circle to the farthest edge, where a spring gurgled up and spilled over into a sluice. The water was inky black and running fast. The forbidding, grey-walled corridor of the sluice led us downwards, until it emerged into a stagnant marsh.

"This is the Styx," said Virgil with a sweep of his arm. I gazed intently, alert for danger. We all know the name 'Styx'! I could hear strange grunts, sharp cries and curious burbling. As my eyes grew accustomed to the dim, I saw more and more people, immersed in that fetid fen. They were peevish, naked, caked with mud and they fought each other vehemently. They slapped, punched, scratched, head-butted, kicked. Some even tore at each other with their teeth. Every now and then, one fell open-mouthed in the slop, and rose again to choke and vomit.

"These allowed anger and wrath to overcome them in the Leave or Remain debate," explained Virgil. "Some had been friends …. before. Some were even from the same family. See what they do to each other now. This is the **Fifth Circle.**"

Oh, what a consuming vice is wrath! How it warps and distorts our very being. I knew what had happened. No more a pleasant evening at the pub. No more a nice chat over coffee on the corner. No more companions, comfortable together in the living room round the TV after a day's work. Lost, the rhythm of cooking together; eating their breakfast in drowsy silence together before an early shift. As I watched, heavy with sadness, I noticed bubbles swell and burst in the black, stinking slime, like a speeded-up video of a ghastly pox. Methane? Here?

"What causes those bubbles?" I asked.

"Those are the hums of the sullen, who turned their anger inward and sulked. They have sunk beneath the surface and gurgle now their sorry tune, gulping the slime," replied Virgil.

3 ACROSS THE STYX

[Canto 8] Keeping close to the hard, grey cliff, we walked on round the edge of this foaming, sour sludge towards a distant pinprick of light that floated in one spot in the night air. As we got nearer, I saw it was a fire signal, lit at the top of a tall stone tower. Once we had arrived at the tower's base, I spotted another similar light, far in the distance, responding.

I turned to my 'fount of all knowledge'. It was becoming a habit. "What have we here, Virgil? Who is responding over there?" I asked.

"This stretch represents your Special Relationship with that place 'across the Pond', as your people call it. Let's go and see," came the reply.

Suddenly a boat shot towards us, like an arrow, from the thick mist hanging above the mire. It looked like a battered, but sea-worthy, fishing boat. The helmsman was shouting with pent-up rage. He seemed to think he had been the victim of a massive hoax.

"What a f***ing mess! The lies, the lies I am finding out now. And I bloody believed them. This is people's livelihoods we're talking about. It shouldn't be allowed."

"Calm down, Phil. Just give us a ride across. We're

paying good money," said Virgil.

As we boarded, Phil the Fisherman shoved nets and floats aside to give us space to sit. I watched the muscles rippling in his back, as he worked, rigid with tension. "Where do we sell it all now, eh? Answer me that one! The f***ers! Where do we sell, for Chrissake? They promised we were taking back control of our waters. Those Frogs and Vikings could no longer come in their swarms and leave nothing for us. Well, great! There's plenty of fish now. Bigger catches, though still less than they promised. That's another thing! Anyway, what's the f***ing use, if we can't sell the stuff like we used to? They never mentioned what it would mean for our sales. Now I am stuck running ferries in this lifeless slick, when I should be out on the fresh, open sea."

Virgil just let the fisherman vent, as he eased the boat back, swung her round and revved her forward into the foaming waves. The noise of the engine churning through the mire soon drowned his ranting. After a couple of minutes, we lost sight of both shores. All I could see to give me some sense of direction was the pinprick of light from the far tower. My eyes struggled to tell if it was actually getting bigger.

Suddenly, a large head reared up from the slime and two strong, but rather dainty, hands clawed at the gunwales. As the black slop slid away, I saw his face clearly. It was strangely orange except for two white panda circles around the eyes, and the heavy jowls hung low on a firm jaw. From under the muck still clinging to his hair, I saw streaks of what must once have been artificially blond.

"You gotta help me get back outta here. They stole it from me," he bellowed, without introduction, his American accent unmistakable. A switch seemed to flip in his eyes as he looked at me. "Who are you? You look like my kind of broad. Good figure. Nice boobs. Intelligent face. You're with us, aren't you? They stole it from me. They stole it." Tears started streaming down his face.

"Oh, I know who YOU are," I responded as I slammed the sharp edge of my shield down on his straining knuckles. "Get back down and weep on, loser!"

With a squeal of pain, he lost his grip. Phil the Fisherman revved the engine again and we surged forward. Looking back, I saw his small hands clutch and grasp the air as his heavy mass dragged him under again.

Virgil looked at me in amused surprise. And then he ringed his arms around my neck and kissed my cheek. I let him. "You angry woman! Blessed the one that bore you", he said. "That man flaunted his arrogance and very little good adorns his memory. A self-deceiver, he acted like a king while in power and sprawled like a swine in this mire, when his term was over. He leaves only a name that most revile."

"But the damage he did lives on," I argued. I could not help myself. "He gave sway to those dogma-driven circus-masters. He made it normal for politicians simply to invent 'facts' that suit their ends. He gave master-classes in manipulation. How to take a genuine and legitimate preoccupation, based in reality, and spin from it an entire conspiracy of lies and half-truths, stoking fear. There are many now who believe only he can save them. He fanned into an inferno the manageable fires of dissatisfaction that should have been addressed and put out with firmly negotiated solutions. Now the fire may be beyond control. Only civil war may satisfy it. May he rot!"

"But why does what may happen in his country bother you so much, Britannia?" asked Virgil. I knew he knew the answer already. But in the spirit of Phil the Fisherman, I allowed myself to vent

"Because the high-drama, soap-opera, dog-whistle political culture he created is addictive. The habit has spread wide and fast. Democracy is decaying. I have seen what happened in my own land. I know the part he played. And I am beginning to see why I am here."

As I finished, we heard a piercing cry behind us. I turned

and saw the vicious slime-slathered hordes in that vile swamp had found our heavy interlocutor and were tearing him apart. I set my eyes forward to the shore ahead and ignored his wails.

[Canto 9] As we approached the shore, a city took form in front of us. Minarets, bell towers and domes all stood out against the red glow that seemed to come from fires within.

"This is the City of Dis," explained Virgil. "The **Sixth Circle** and the gateway to the inner circles of Hell."

His face looked paler and more drawn than I had ever seen it. Buoyed by my first proactive intervention in the swamp and my dawning understanding of what I was seeking here, I, on the other hand, refused to pay any attention to the knot of apprehension in my stomach. There are times when a brave face is needed, even if foolish.

The boat eased around the shore from which the city walls rose up, hard and black as iron. Then the graffiti started: swear words, drawings of male and female genitalia, swastika's, the circled 'A' of anarchy. The shore was at first just a narrow strip of bare, dry mud. But as we progressed, the first few bags of discarded rubbish gave way to piles of stinking refuse. A rusted fridge with its door hanging off, a mattress ripped wide open, covered with black bags spilling their harlequin guts of old clothes, rotting vegetable peelings, a doll's head, a half-gnawed bone of meat, an upside-down shoe with a hole in the sole, a cylinder head, bulging plastic shopping bags that I would certainly never dare open, rustling as the rats scuttled among them. The dank air from the swamp hung over us. Just as the city's glow spilled on to the shore a few hundred meters ahead, the graffiti on the iron walls gave way to full-scale murals of the torture of saints in vivid accuracy, lit by the security spotlights on the walls.

The glow intensified, where a massive arch in the wall took shape. It framed a vast crowd, milling, like worker ants, at its base. They moved in and out of what looked to me to be a city on fire.

"Out you get," shouted Phil the Fisherman, as our bow drove up onto the mud and the boat stalled. "Here's the entrance". Virgil moved forward and shoved a plank from the bow to the shore. I put on my helmet, grabbed my shield and followed. Phil took my hand to steady me and Virgil stretched his forward to meet me. Holding my head high, I thanked Phil for his service and descended. I noticed he was most anxious not to get off the boat. As soon as we were on dry land, Phil re-started the engine and revved hard in reverse, while Virgil tilted the plank back in and gave a shove to the bows. I leant in too, eager to show willing. The boat receded.

I turned and, at that precise moment, there was an ear-splitting explosion from within the city. Figures ran out through the arch, overtaken by a few tiny fragments of shrapnel.

Amid the shrieks I heard a man's voice shout: "Another bloody school bus blown up!". I looked to see if anyone was hurt, but I don't quite know what I would have done if they had been.

As the melee subsided, faces began to turn towards us. They were not welcoming. My feet felt impaled to the muddy beach. If only my cloak could make me invisible.

"What's she doing here?" hissed a wizened old woman, wrapped in a filthy brown blanket. "She ain't dead?" Others turned to stare at us.

"Yeah, who are you?" "What's your business here?" they called.

Virgil stood tall. He seemed to glow. Leaning forward very slightly, he inclined his head and simply said "We shall pass" with a mild smile. "Our business is none of yours."

At that moment, an other-worldly shrieking rent the air, far more piercing than anything we had heard before, accompanied by a strange rushing sound. In panic, every person in the crowd shielded their eyes with their hands and hunched over. Some dived for cover back through the arch, like frogs who glimpse a heron. They slammed the vast, heavy doors.

My gaze was drawn to the top of the arch. There perched three blood-stained creatures. They were shaped like women, but instead of hair, their heads were a mass of writhing, bright green venomous snakes. The snakes seemed to be pushing their way out through the follicles, some further emerged than others, like blow-fly maggots when daubed with oil. The creatures slapped their own breasts and tore at the skin with their nails, shrieking. Each shriek exposed their sharp, blackened teeth, also smeared with blood.

These I recognized: the Furies; led by Medusa to avenge the murdered. A wave of foreboding swept over me at the sight of these creatures and what their presence might mean awaited us, should we succeed in passing through this arch.

"Turn your back to them and cover your eyes," shouted Virgil, barely audible over their shrieking. "If the Gorgon appears and you see her, there'll be no way of ever getting you out of here."

I obeyed and felt Virgil's hands close over mine for double insurance. As I waited, he moved away. I risked a small peek through my fingers to check what he was doing. After all, my back was still turned to the shrieking Furies. Their tone had not changed, so I guessed the Gorgon had not yet arrived.

Virgil's head was turned, looking into the distance along the shore. His eyes swung quickly back to check that the Furies had not moved from their perch and then resumed their search into the putrid black fog above that nauseous swamp.

"What are you expecting?" I asked.

"More, who?" he replied, distracted.

At that moment, a huge, muscled figure emerged. His left fore-arm was raised, pushing away the greasy fog, like a fireman moving through a burning building, as his right fore-arm fanned a pathway. He plodded forwarded at a steady pace and I saw that his feet were staying dry. I looked at Virgil for an answer. He merely indicated that I should show some respect with a small bow. The man or demi-god paused as he stepped on the shore. From the corner of my eye as I bent my head, I saw him nod at Virgil and glance at me down his long aquiline nose. I heard him sniff. Then he turned towards the city gates. The Furies squawked and vanished from their perch into the night.

"You recalcitrant scum," he called to the crowds inside, sighing as though he had had to do this too often, although I thought that was unlikely. "What makes you so truculent? Why kick against your fate? You cannot block the way for these two. It is ordained." And with that he simply pushed open the city gates with a small staff. They were not even barred.

He then turned back and set out again across the swamp, heavy with care. That was it. Not even an adieu or good luck. Virgil said nothing and his expression made me hold my tongue, though I was dying to know who this character was.

Instead, Virgil pressed forward, and I followed closely, with some trepidation. However, inside the gates, there was no teeming, menacing crowd, no tangled streets, choked gutters and bustling busy-ness, as I had imagined. No explosions. No buses or transport of any kind. No need to watch your back. Instead, we stood on the edge of a wide plain, dotted with stone tombs, each with flames prancing in a pit beside it. The fires were intense, far hotter than any farrier would need. The cover of each tomb lay half removed and from each tomb drifted agonising cries of pain.

Wincing, I turned to Virgil, "Who are the people entombed here? What have they done to be condemned to this?"

"They are the worshippers of false dogma - the heretics - and their followers. They sacrificed Truth and the post-World War II consensus for European peace on the altar of

Sovereignty. They split their own party in two and forced a hard line. To some they are known as the 'ERG'. They are more in total than appears, because each tomb is packed: like minds with like, and all at different temperatures."

[Canto 10] He turned right and we followed a small path along the curve of the high walls; the wailing tombs always on our left side. Suddenly, one cry rang out louder than the others and startled me. I spotted immediately a man with the top half of his body, protruding from the sepulchre, thin and pasty with long, dark chest hairs. He placed some round wire-framed glasses on his nose and called: "Britannia, at last." His tone was surprisingly imperious, as if entitled to my attention. "I am awfully glad to see you've come," he added.

Virgil waved me forward. I approached to the edge of the man's raised tomb, from where he looked down on me.

"Thank goodness, you're here," he said, conspiratorially. "We stood up for you then and now we could do with a spot of assistance here."

"What do you mean?" I enquired, without emotion.

"Oh, come on! We pushed a jolly hard line to stand up for your sovereignty against those Brussels bureaucrats and continentals. You simply can't trust them. Always trying to limit everything without our consent. We even managed to outwit all those BINO's in our own party - you know, Brexit-In-Name-Only. Cowards, the lot of them!" He giggled. "Now our global power will be unfettered. Total sovereignty, like the days of Empire."

"Empire, you say?" I responded. "Do I need to remind you that we are no longer in the nineteenth century? Did we not have global power already last month?" I caught a glimpse of surprise in his eyes, though he kept smiling. I continued: "Doesn't 'global power' mean the ability to project one's influence far beyond one's own borders? Was the European Union not the biggest trading bloc in the world, negotiating complex trade deals to our advantage around the world? And had we not painstakingly built friction-less trade with our largest and nearest trading partner?"

"But we don't need them. We can do it alone. Everything we did within the EU we can do alone.... and more. Above all, we have sovereignty back for you, Britannia. We'll make our own decisions."

"Sovereignty! I am seriously weakened. I feel it in my whole body."

"But only temporarily. A minor inconvenience in the longer term. You'll see," he interrupted.

"Name me one ally that admires what you have done? Name me one country with which we will have a more valuable trading relationship than we had from within the EU?"

"Oh, they're queueing up. It may take a little time to build up, but we have your dignity and sovereignty back. We have taken back control. Stopped the rot. Buck up, Britannia, this is not like you. You sound like you've been listening too much to the merchant class, if I may say so. They'll be alright. They'll look after themselves. They always do. You and I don't need to worry about them. It's your sovereignty and dignity that matter."

"'Sovereignty', again! 'Dignity' again! Just what do you mean by those words? Why do I feel weaker? Every agreement with another nation entails some limiting of your own room for manoeuvre thereafter. But you choose to do it where the benefit is greater than the sacrifice/cost. That's what every international agreement – for trade or otherwise - entails. Why am I now scorned or mocked by many of our important allies?"

His face began to betray just a little hurt, but he laughed and raised his hands.

"We've taken back control of decision making. They're just sore losers, because we thought of it first," he claimed triumphantly, as if we were facing up in the school playground. "We'll set our own rules, our own standards, which we regulate, judged by our own courts," he continued, raising his oratorical tone to the levels of pomposity.

"Are you not confusing notional autonomy with real power?" I asked. "Will our financial sector keep growing as it has, unless we maintain the standards the EU set?"

"Oh, but the EU'll agree to us joining back in with the financial system. After all, we're world leaders." He began to re-find his stride.

"And if we do, and continue to meet the standards they set, now and in the future, what was the point in leaving the EU? How do I, Britannia, gain power from that, eh?"

"They need us. They'll give in. We'll set new standards ourselves. Ones that are even better for us. You're beginning to sound like one of those bloody BINO's. Above all we have your honour and your sovereignty back. You should be thanking me for that." He frowned.

"What purpose does your so-called 'sovereignty' serve if it makes me weaker economically, politically and even culturally in reality? Is it not over-simplified, verging-on-xenophobic nationalism? Do you think I am so weak that I lose my identity when I stand shoulder-to-shoulder with my friends?"

"But the European Union is fundamentally undemocratic. The voices of the smaller nations are severely over-represented. The Maltese man on the street has a greater say than your own citizens, Britannia. That's undemocratic; even anti-democratic," he argued.

"You do have a point there," I agreed. "But did accumulating our allies' and our own 'sovereignty' in a united front not also enhance our global power? Like I said, we are no longer in the nineteenth century. Domination by force is no longer the path. Peace nourishes prosperity. Medium-sized nations, like us, are we not stronger when we stand together? Aren't our voices louder in chorus than solo? I know you meant well. But that is not enough. You foolish man-boy! If the representation is unbalanced, why not argue that out with the other members, rather than stomping out of the club altogether? Now we must remain bound by many of the rules, if we want to continue trading with them, but we have no say at all in what those rules are. How does that make me stronger? While you are here, you might think about that."

I turned and walked back to our path, where Virgil stood patiently waiting.

"Wait a minute, Britannia. We did all this for you", he whined behind me. "You can't just abandon us here. What's got into you? We've taken back control for you. Now do your bit and get us out."

His voice, ever more desperate, began to fade as the flames began to rise higher. I could feel the heat on my back.

We walked on in silence, still following the wall, to a point where Virgil swung left on a small path, which took us straight towards the centre. It cut down into a gorge. Even from the top, the foul smell was overpowering.

[Canto 11] We stood at the brink of a steep scarp slope, formed in enormous concentric circles of huge shattered rocks and descending into a seemingly bottom-less funnel. The rock walls glowed with heat from fire and I could hear tortured cries of unimaginable pain. From the depths of the abyss below, belched up a stench so vile we had to take shelter behind the cover of one of the tombs at the edge of the plain we had just crossed. Despite myself, I retched.

"Let us pause to get a little accustomed to this smell before we continue," offered Virgil. Relieved, I nodded agreement. Not wishing to seem weak, I added:

"While we wait, please explain to me where we are. So we use our time wisely."

Virgil thought for a moment and then began:

"Within this grim pit lie three Circles, going gradually deeper, like the ones we have already passed through. Each is packed with cursed souls, as before. Listen now to the 'how' and 'why' of their particular punishment. In this way, your eyes alone will be enough later on.

"Malice, in all its forms, aims to create injustice. It does so either by force or by deceit. But deceit is even worse than force, because it is specifically a human wrong. I shall explain. The **Seventh Circle**, the first we enter here, is dedicated to acts of violence. Violence takes three main forms and each of these can be committed on people or their property. So, this Circle itself is sub-divided into three: first, violence to others, both their person or their property. Secondly, violence to yourself, including those who dissipate the things they have of worth with waste or gambling, for example – or any act of self-harm, even economic. And thirdly, those who commit violence on the Truth.

"As for deceit, this turns to malicious and destructive ends the very gifts that set humans apart from other animals in Nature - namely, the gifts of reason and rational speech. Deceit uses them to abuse our fellow human beings. For this reason, the **Eighth and Ninth Circles** are where you will find the worst torture and suffering.

In the many separate trenches in the **Eighth Circle**, you will encounter those who committed various forms of fraud on their fellow humans. They misinformed or deliberately fooled others with lies and half-truths. Here are the pimps and seducers, the flatterers, those who sold official positions and benefits, the false prophets, the corrupt officials and politicians, the hypocrites, the thieves, those who gave false counsel, the rabble-rousers who spread division, and, lastly, the falsifiers.

"But the **Ninth Circle** – the point in the universe where Satan sits – is reserved for those who deceived people who trusted them and had cause to trust them. Here are the worst of the worst, consumed eternally: the traitors, who betray special bonds. They have betrayed their family, their guests or their colleagues, their own benefactors and/or their nation. And some, as you will see, have betrayed more than one of these in multiple deeds."

He paused. His explanation had held my attention, but now another wave of the stench from below washed over me and slid down my throat. I retched again, bent double, gagging and heaving. I felt Virgil's concerned eyes on my back. I held my arm and hand aloft behind me to indicate I did not need help and had something to ask. After dabbing away the slime from my chin, I pulled myself up.

"Thank you, thank you. Your explanation is very clear. But all those souls in that putrid marsh above us now, the pitiful creatures lashed by icy rain, and the stone-pushers who clash with such abrasive tongues, they are all in Hell too. So why not here within these flame-red walls?" I asked.

"Have your wits become so frayed, they wander from the reasoned track, Britannia? Or have your thoughts fled elsewhere to more pleasant surroundings? Think of your education, even from those who wrote in the times I lived," he responded.

"Ah Virgil, you are the sun which heals all clouded sight," I smiled weakly, to encourage him to go on and nibbled on some dry bread from the pouch strapped to my waist.

"Those in the Fifth Circle and from there back up, all have vices that stem from self-indulgence - self-centredness and lack of self-control - more than from deliberate malice," he continued. "Think of Aristotle's teachings and the early Christians."

Lust, gluttony, avarice, wrath: lack of self-control, indeed. That is certainly different from intentional violence, fraud and betrayal. I decided not to quibble over the worshippers of false dogma (the heretics) in the Sixth Circle.

Virgil was looking ahead and fidgeting. My stomach had settled sufficiently. Time to move on.

[Canto 12] Ahead of us the ground dropped like an alpine crag. We clambered and slid down a scree of boulders, probably triggered by an earthquake or landslide. As we picked our way, the stones often rocked underfoot and

turned. By the time we reached the bottom, my ankles and feet were bruised and three of my toes were bleeding. But our attention was fixed on the vast ditch, which arc-ed to embrace the plain. A flow of steaming vermillion raced along it. High-pitched shrieks of pain erupted from the figures floating in it; at least, from those with their mouths above the surface. Centaurs cantered up and down, firing arrows at any who tried to escape the river's drag. The stench we had encountered at the top of the pass enveloped us still.

"This is the river of boiling blood. Here simmer all those whose violence damaged others. They are tyrants who lent their hands to blood for violent gain," explained Virgil.

As we made our way along the shore, he pointed out the heads of Alexander the Great and Attila the Hun, yelling with pain. But my eye was caught by another, his muscled, naked torso clearly showing above the flow, a little downstream. He appeared to be on horse-back, the horse's head also above the flow just ahead of him. He must have reached a sand bank underwater as he rose further, closer now. A rifle was slung over his shoulder, washed in red. He was not a big man, but what strength of body and mind must have been required to be navigating this river on horseback without anguish? Thin remains of fine blond hair were matted with dried blood. But it was his eyes I recognized: of steel, steady, pale and cold. I recalled the words of another who had looked into them before me and remarked he saw no soul. He had received but a smile in return. Without a soul, this place could cause no pain. I had heard about his schemes to steer our vote via internet groups and weaken Europe to his own strategic advantage. This one was smarter than to use violence alone. I did not stop to confirm his Russian accent, and had no need to know him better. Trusting I could move faster on land than he in that viscous flow, I stretched my stride to catch up with Virgil.

Some way ahead, the river became shallow enough to

stew only the toes of those damned to bathe in it. At Virgil's request, one of the centaur's carried us across.

[Canto 13] We began to travel through a strange wood. There was no path so I had to trust in Virgil's sense of direction. The trees were dense, contorted, knotted and entwined. The leaves were a murky brown. Instead of bright fruit, the boughs bore poison-tipped thorns. The tangled ramshackle nests of Harpies were festooned in the higher branches of many. An acrid smell wafted up from the sticky guano underfoot. At least it counter-acted the nauseating stench I had suffered from earlier. The Harpies stood on their nests above us, wings spread, like cormorants drying after a fishing expedition. From neck to brow, they had a human form, but plumage covered their swollen paunches and their feet were talons. They sang tuneless dirges of woe.

Virgil urged me to look around, away from the Harpies. "If I were to tell you what you will see here, you would not believe me," he said. I could hear a wailing that seemed to come from every side, but not from the Harpies. Yet I could not see any persons or things which might make that noise. I stood, bewildered. Where were they hiding?

"Try tearing off a sprig from any tree," said Virgil. I did. It was just a small shoot, I swear, which looked pretty dry and dead anyway.

"Why gash me so? We were once men. Have you no pity?" moaned a voice in the tree, it seemed. I dropped the shoot and jumped back, horror-struck. The wood at the point where I had snapped off the shoot was a deep red, and, with each word, large crimson drops fell from the shoot in my hand. Virgil, on the other hand, showed no surprise at all.

"You injured soul!" he said, addressing the tree of red wood. "Tell us your story."

"I was so sure," said the voice, converting the light wind into words. "In the beginning, I believed that European leaders were not tackling the zone's underlying economic problems. I was so sure we would be better off outside the European Union. We needed to take back control. I believed we held most of the cards. European companies would be dead set against losing their markets in the UK. We would get a good exit deal. And when the signs were there, that a vote to leave could be an act of economic self-harm, I shouted down those nay-sayers. I threatened business leaders with disruption to their corporate governance if they spoke of their concerns. Regardless of economic analysis, I told them to stay out of political debate. I pushed ahead. I believed we could overcome any risks to investment from leaving the European Union. We had to take back control of our borders and all decisions that promote or hinder our economic growth; regain our sovereignty. But underneath, I knew. I knew. I knew that this would cause us harm. Oh woe!"

"I appreciate your concern for my sovereignty," I said in an effort to show some mercy to this pitiful wretch. But I could not sustain it. "You have some friends, frying in tombs, not far from here. So you are not alone in your woe. Tell me, how could you think we held good cards, with more than 40% of all our exports going to the EU – 75% of our fish exports - while less than 10% of EU exports came in the other direction?" I asked.

The voice was silent. Four Harpies flew in and landed on its crown, where they started pecking at the foliage. The moans of pain resumed, in chorus with others in this ghastly wood.

Just then, a sudden uproar surprised us. A hunt! Baying dogs and some large beast crashing through the brush, coming our way. A human figure, naked, torn, filled with the energy of terror, burst from the undergrowth on our left. The full-throated barks of the hounds were closing in on us. Virgil and I dived behind two tree trunks and peeked around. Have you ever felt the primordial rush of being chased by a pack of hounds in full cry, leaping and baying, driving forward with one end in mind? Although I knew mine was not the scent they followed, I did not intend to distract them.

The man glanced over his shoulder and then took three strides more and hunched down into a thorny bush, as if he hoped to be absorbed by it. His flash of thick, white hair sat among the twigs, like cotton ready for harvest. But his scent betrayed him. Six lithe, black hounds exploded through the undergrowth, like buckshot from a gun, and leaped upon him. They seized and tore with razor teeth. Their claws dug deep in the ground as they set their entire weight and strength into pulling him apart. I looked away, but my gaze was drawn back by unseen chords. The hounds were quiet now and started to disperse, each dragging some part of the wretch's body.

Virgil stepped forward and gently led me to the bush, which had begun to weep blood quietly. "So, who were you, so pierced to bits?" he asked softly.

"I told them. I did, I told them. As a newly sovereign nation, we can make trade deals bilaterally with each of you. That's what I told each EU member. Done and dusted within two years. No problem. I knew their corporate titans would be banging down their political leaders' doors, demanding unfettered access to our markets. You don't have to be a genius to see where their interests lay."

"Are you the one who claimed 'There will be no downsides, only upsides'?" I asked.

"Indeed, I did. And so it could have been, if they had not insisted on putting politics above prosperity. Never a smart choice."

"Was that not exactly what you were doing?" I asked. "Are you the one who edited reports that forecast damaging economic effects from a vote to leave the EU to be less negative? Reports commissioned by the government you were a part of."

"Ends justify means sometimes."

"And the result? Has it not been called the biggest conscious act of economic self-harm ever committed by a nation?" I cried.

"No, no. It was more complicated than that. They were the ones who put politics above prosperity. They insisted that frictionless trade could not come without freedom of movement of people. They all stood together. It could have been different."

"You foolish man! It seems you need time here to understand what you have done," I said. "Even your own party realized you were not competent to do the job allotted to you. They side-lined you in favour of a civil servant with sharper brains to get the real work done."

I turned away, ready to move on. But a small part of me could not leave one of my people in such distress. I gathered up the leaves strewn around him and returned them to the bush. I saw the expression on Virgil's face. Accomplished warrior you may be, Britannia, but there is no room for sentimentality, if you are to surpass the ordeals to come.

[Canto 14 & 15] From there, we reached the boundary between the second and third - the last - ring within the **Seventh Circle.** The wood fringed a barren plain of coarse, dry sand, too hot and arid for any form of vegetation. Dotted around the plain were naked human figures. Some lay supine on the ground. Some sat huddled, knees drawn up, wrapped tightly in their arms. Most strode around. All wept mournfully. Wind-whipped sand scoured their skin. Much worse, large flakes of fire drifted down, like snow, but mercilessly burning. Without rest, the figures brushed and slapped the flakes from their skin, in a surreal hand jive. But even from where I stood, I could see the fire had branded their limbs. Where flakes landed on the ground, the sand caught fire, like tinder under flint, and doubled the pain from underfoot.

I started forward to see if I could identify any of the sufferers.

"Stop there!" cried Virgil. "Do not set foot on those blistering sands. The soles of your shoes will be scorched straight through. Keep to the edge. We go around."

"But who is there?" I asked. "I recall you said that this third Ring is for those who did violence to the Truth, but I must see who has found their end here."

"No, you cannot step there," responded Virgil. "In any case, they are too many. All those who campaigned for Brexit using incomplete and deliberately misleading and false arguments are here. But don't worry. We will find their leaders even deeper down, because their guilt is more thoroughly steeped in intent."

In silence, we moved on until we came to a steaming, bubbling stream, spurting from the woods. I still squirm as I remember its vivid redness. So bright, the flame flakes above it dimmed. It promised only evil. But it ran across the flaming plain and burning sands in the direction we needed. And it coursed along a wide, stone-sided gutter. The vapours floating up from it quenched those flame flakes. Its banks offered the only safe path for us. As we walked, I began to hear a rumble, like a bee-hive, that gradually increased in volume.

4 DELVING THE DITCHES OF DECEPTION

[Canto 16 & 17] We reached the edge of the plain and the scarlet river plunged over a precipice, thundering with such a force it hurt my ears. Virgil asked me to remove the knotted cord I wore across my left shoulder and pass it to him. Unwinding it to its full length, he then gathered it in even coils, twirled it three times like a lasso and flung one end over the cliff edge into the swirling, steaming torrent and braced his legs to avoid following it. I know you may not believe me, but I swear I saw a figure swimming up the cascade. As it crested the cliff, it launched its top half on to the bank a little way below us.

"Behold! The beast who soars with needle tail. The beast who stinks out all the world. The Monster of Deceit!" cried Virgil. The smell was nauseating. The same foul odour we had been suffering all the way through the Seventh Circle, only now no longer mixed with the acrid smoke of burning flesh and earth. But my senses were more focused on the appearance of the creature in front of us, half-beached on the stony bank. The face was that of any man and looked honest and generous. But below the shoulders, its torso was covered in multi-coloured tattoos of knots and whorls, which masked a transition from human to reptilian skin. Its lower body was a serpent. At the end of its arms were grabbing claws, not hands. And as it heaved itself forward like a vast walrus, it swung its tail up above the water: forked and tipped with venomous scorpion stings.

Treading carefully, so as not to alarm it, we advanced. Ten paces and we had reached the very edge of the gaping chasm. To one side, I now noticed a sandbar with three figures crouched on it, swatting at the flaming flakes which fell through the gap in the torrent's vapours. Virgil urged me to go and speak with them while he would negotiate with the monster for safe passage to the next level. Getting closer, I saw their pain in deep, black holes in their eyes. Like dogs in a heat-wave, tormented by flies and fleas, they swatted and twitched. Their bodies were patched with old burn scars and lurid new wounds. I did not recognize any of them fully, but the faces of two of the three were somewhat familiar from the band whose leader I had spoken to in the Sixth Circle, as he stood in his cooking tomb. One was muttering the words "Take Back Control" over and over like a bass mantra. Another, repeated "Vote Leave. We will still have the Single Market. Frictionless trade." And the third suddenly howled a high pitch "Sovereignty". Then he wrenched his mouth awry and curled his immense tongue upwards like an ox to lick the inside of his left nostril. I was anxious not to delay further our journey to the heart of the matter. There is a limit to how much pain one can witness without becoming deadened and blunt. So I turned my back on these wretched souls.

To my horror, I saw Virgil was now sitting astride that ghastly creature's rump. In front of him, it unfolded and flexed huge wings. "Come on," he cried. "Muster that famous courage of yours, Britannia, and join me here. We cannot descend to the next Circles without aid. Get on in front of me, so I can protect you from the tail tip in case of accidents."

Shaking and pale, as if I had the flu, I placed my hand on the stinking creature's back. I knew I had no choice. The force of Virgil's trust and expectation for this mission, that depended on me alone, both strengthened me and shamed me into ignoring my dread and disgust.

I swung my leg over and immediately felt two firm arms embrace my waist tightly from behind me. "Go then!" he cried to the monster. "Cast out, wheel wide and give us a smooth descent. Remember the burden on your back."

Ferry-style, we slithered astern. But as soon as we were floating free, the simile ended. The monster curled his body round and stretched forward, elongating like an eel, and launched himself – and us - into the void, soaring and paddling the air towards him with his claws. After one brief glance downwards, which made my head swim so that I nearly passed out, I kept my eyes fixed on the intricate patterns of the tattoos on the monster's back in front of me and my legs locked around his body. A slight movement between my thighs and the wind fanning my face signalled that we were in descent. Shrill screams assailed my ears and from the corners of my eyes, I caught glimpses of fires dotted in the blackness. I leaned back and felt Virgil's arms close tighter around me.

The monster started to glide in ever tighter circles and landed with disdain, the way a falcon resists return to an empty-handed falconer. We slid stiffly from his back and stood at the foot of a towering cliff. He vanished, like a barbed bolt from a bow.

[Canto 18] The towering, circular cliff walls at our backs and the rock beneath our feet were uniformly the colour of rusted iron. In the centre of the malign plain ahead yawned a wide well. Between us and that central pit lay ten concentric trenches, forming the figure of a wheel around it, like a series of moats guarding an inverted castle keep. Each moat was spanned by radial stone bridges, one after

another, like spokes to the wheel, until they were swallowed into the central hub.

"Welcome to the **Eighth Circle**," said Virgil and set off to the left. I followed. On my right in the first trench, I saw fresh suffering: new torments and new torturers. Down in the depths, stark naked, a stream of sinners hurried with their faces turned upwards to us. On the far side, another row moved in the other direction, even faster. Dotted around the rocks, horned demons, armed with vicious whips, struck at the sinners. At the first lash, they scurried forward. No-one waited for second servings. Several arched their backs to evade the whip and threw their heads back. At that moment, my eyes connected with the eyes of one.

"I know that one!" I cried. "I have seen him before." I stopped and took a few steps back to be in front of him again.

The slim, stooping body was badly beaten. He quickly turned his head down, as if he thought he had a hood to pull over his balding pate to avoid detection.

"You there!" I shouted. "Eyes-down! Bashful, are you? I know your profile: that high hairless forehead and deep-set eyes. Do they need testing again? Your casual look, your loping stride and air of the Grim Reaper does not work here, does it? No clothes to leave untucked. Which of your many sins brings you to this particular trench?"

"Yes, I fixed it. I knew from the start that the Big Blond was unfit to govern. But he was a vote-winner. Every fool could see that! We considered it worth a roll of the dice. We reckoned we could rein him in and keep him on our track, once elected. So, I used my talents to put him forward and seduce the voters. Fed him lines; he knew how to deliver them. I pimped him straight. We kept it up for a long while. It wasn't actually easy. He's an ignorant and lazy whore, despite the ebullience. But unlike most of those here in this ditch, I didn't do it for money. I did it to save that sclerotic country from its own decline."

I listened in amazement. But he had not finished.

Speaking faster now, as he spotted one of the demons approaching, he continued: "It was a weird opportunity to push through certain important things that the system wouldn't do, left to itself. Precisely because he didn't know what he was doing, we could achieve what was necessary. Until the system caught up with us." He started shuffling forward, head down again.

"And then you abandoned him."

"I owe him nothing," he fired back and leapt forward, just as the demon's scourge landed on his back, tearing at the soft flesh. He howled, but clearly not with repentance.

"Push off, you pimp!" screeched the demon.

Somehow, I had not expected to see him among the prostitutes' pimps. I had never associated him with the seedier side of carnal lust. But, reflecting on his words his situation made sense. Still, a part of me thought he had surely committed even worse sins. Did he not belong even lower in Hell? But I did not have time to resolve that now. I turned to join Virgil once again and walked a few steps further by his side, until we reached a rocky outcrop, which jutted from the bank. We made our way up it quite easily and continued until we were right over the middle of the trench. From there we looked down on the figures passing in the other direction, also driven by the whistling whips.

"You know enough about this trench and those caught in its fangs," said Virgil and moved on across the bridge. He seemed to be in a hurry. Beats me why.

Straight across from the bottom the one bridge, another began, spanning the second trench. As we ascended, we heard the groans and griping of another lot, along with snuffles of snouts and slapping of palms. The smell was appalling. I held a corner of my cloak over my mouth. The banks were crusted with slime and mould, fed by the vapours rising from the flowing sludge deep below. All the sinners here were plunged in diarrhoea – their own, I guessed.

Scanning back and forth, I spotted one whose head was

so encrusted in excrement, I could not identify him by his face and hair. But, unlike the other naked creatures, this one still had what must once have been a silky pink tie around his neck. How he had kept that, I could not know. Perhaps it had proved impossible to remove.

He noticed my gaze and shouted up, "Why are you gawping at me like that? What's wrong with the other swill?"

"Because I have seen you before … with drier hair," I replied. "Tell me why you have landed here."

"I'm sunk this deep because of flatteries. None were too sickly for me. When those ahead of me in the power game took a different view to my first instincts, I simply changed tack and flattered them to believe their wisdom had helped me see the errors in my judgment. I always bounced back. And thus I bounced my way to the governing table. First, I sweet-talked the Thin One. After the Vote, I was one of the very few politicians who voted to Remain, but was nevertheless appointed to govern. When the Thin One fell, I contested the party leadership. But when I saw the Big Blond would beat me, I withdrew. Perhaps I had not flattered enough Bigwigs. Instead, I backed him and persuaded him that he had shown me the True Path and I would be a loyal follower. His ego is so swollen, it was not difficult."

"And did it end there?" I asked.

"No, oh no. I am sure you recall the arguments about what kind of deal could be accepted. I was sure that leaving the EU without a deal was not a policy option, whether our leader liked it or not. I said so publicly in no uncertain terms. To the people who said 'f*** business', I said f*** 'f*** business'. But when it looked like a parliamentary vote to stop a so-called 'no-deal exit' could not succeed, I said I had changed my mind. I had to lick a lot of shit to persuade them of my loyalty. But Hell, the one thing I did well was brown-nosing. And so you see me here."

He paused. I glanced at Virgil. He stood with a fold of his robe over his nose and mouth against the stench. Pink

Tie continued: "But surely you, Britannia, can get me out of here. If anyone can, it must be you. So wise and powerful…"

"Let that be all we need to view here," interrupted Virgil and turned to continue over the bridge to the next one. I followed without hesitation.

[*Canto 19*] And so we reached the peak of the next bridge. Oh, sordid crowd! Positions that carry great civic responsibility, the trappings of office, items that should be held as sacred – the brides of Honour and Goodness – were sold by this crowd for filthy lucre, turned into trinkets to satisfy their lust for power. In Christian circles, they call it 'simony': the sale of religious positions and benefits in return for money.

The rock sides and floor of the trench below us had been drilled with identical, circular holes. From every hole, naked legs were sticking out, feet upwards, visible to the tops of the thighs, wiggling like a cockroach's antennae. The rest of their body was crammed into the hole, head first. The soles of the feet had been set alight. Their wriggling only served to fan the flames.

It was impossible to identify them by their legs alone, nor to hear their story. But I was very familiar with 'cash for honours' scandals and the selling of peerages for a minimum donation to political parties – lately as much as three million pounds. The only thing that shocked me was just how many souls were damned to this trench.

"Do you have a message for them?" asked Virgil.

It only took me a moment to channel my feelings and express them in words.

"May you suffer long. You have abased the offices you held. You and your selfish greed bring misery to the world, trampling the good, while raising up and ennobling the wicked. Each one works its insidious blight, steadily eroding public trust in the institutions of government, taking us closer to a collapse of democracy. You have made silver and gold your gods at the expense of the electorate who put their trust in you. I reject you."

Their feet flapped, either in protest and anger or, perhaps remorse, though I doubt it. They would not still be here if they were truly remorseful. Virgil, on the other hand, looked pleased, watching me, his lips compressed. After my final words, he embraced me and lifted me from the ground. No words were said. To my surprise, he turned and carried me from there, clasped to his breast, all the way to the top of a steep, rocky crag which spanned both trenches **Four and Five**. There, he put me gently on the ground and we stood side by side to gaze into the depths below.

[Canto 20] Their faces wet, these sunken souls were circling solemnly in a lake of tears. As my gaze moved down their bodies, I noticed that the angle of chin to chest was distorted. In fact, the whole face was twisted round to face their kidneys. Since they could not see forwards, they had to walk backwards. Agonizing teardrops ran down their spines and trickled into the cleavage of their buttocks. My eyes began to well up with pity, though I knew they did not deserve it. I steadied myself against the hard, jagged rock beside me.

"Are you, Britannia, to show yourself as foolish as them?" said Virgil. "Here walk the occult soothsayers, diviners and false prophets. Lift your head! Stand straight and see that one there. He was at the heart of all this." I watched a forlorn figure approach. With his baby face and slightly jutting lower lip, large eyes magnified by heavy black-framed spectacles, he looked no more uneasy with this distorted body than he had in life.

"Charisma he lacked," said Virgil, "and knew it. But he is clever and used his brains to organize the campaign and spread false messages about future opportunities and magnificent benefits, both tangible and conceptual, that would be seized outside the European Union. He sacrificed Truth to Ideology. See now how he is forced to shuffle backwards to perceive the future."

"Ah yes," I said. "He was another who claimed that 'the day after we leave, we hold all the cards and can choose the path we want'. He was the one who claimed there would be tariff-free trade with the rest of Europe and minimal bureaucracy and a quick deal with the United States on top. He was the one who claimed that Britain would at last be free to liberalise, innovate and grow; that we would not suffer economically, but rather the reverse, ridiculing the advice of many economic experts. Now it is he who walks in reverse. I bet he didn't envisage this, even during his wildest trips in the days he indulged in powerful drugs."

As he neared, I heard him mutter "The Scottish fish, the Scottish fish. I did it for my Dad. How was I to know?"

Virgil called to him and he peered up, though clearly the movement caused his distorted neck considerable pain. He stopped, shocked.

"Britannia!", he cried. "I did it for you. To take back control. To make the union stronger. Outside the EU, Scottish independence is not viable."

At that moment, I felt the old aching in my limbs, as if they were being stretched and torn on the rack, though nothing had changed in my surroundings. I groaned and clung to the rock beside me.

"Was it you who said the union of the United Kingdom and Northern Ireland would be stronger on leaving the EU?" I said, pushing the words through gritted teeth.

"How was I to know that Scotland and Northern Ireland would disagree?" he said.

"You called on the electorate to believe the vision you painted. You sold false, easy solutions to people desperate for relief from grinding problems which were largely created by your own government over the previous decade. You did not mention that, did you? Problems to find jobs, housing, social care, transport, education. People cried for change. But did they even know what they were really voting for? Where are those new free trade deals for 'Global Britain', now unleashed from the so-called deadening fetters of the European Union? With India, China and America? Or even any new trade deals? All I see is time spent replicating deals bilaterally which are no better than the ones we already had as a member of the EU. 'Roll-over', I believe it's called. It seems to me that you have rolled over. Even the new deal with Australia, which should be a no-brainer, is phasing in slowly, because it looks as though it may prove less positive than hoped for British businesses and farmers. The scheme to support those farmers – good as it may be – is not yet ready."

"Ah, you see! You admit there's an improvement. I was responsible for that." He chirped quickly. "How was I to know how long it would take and what things would cost?"

"Now you ask how you were to know? Where is the GBP350 million per week you promised would be returned and given to the health service? That would have been eighteen billion pounds per year. The cost to the economy of leaving will be far higher. It has started to show already."

"How was I to know?" he whined, interrupting me.

"How were you to know? Even your own government advisers warned that the cost would be four percent of gross domestic product annually. That is about eighty billion pounds, compared to the eighteen billion you said would be saved. But you ridiculed them."

"If only they had believed in what we could do," he pleaded pathetically. But I was getting into my stride, surprised by my own vitriol.

'How many of the EU's regulatory constraints that you so railed against have been ditched? Many are being maintained because they do in fact protect public health in valuable ways. You have even defended them yourself. Others are maintained, because you want to continue to trade with the EU and they will not accept lower standards. The rest, who knows?

"And security! You sought to frighten people before the vote with exaggerated claims that it could not be in our

50

security interests to open visa-free travel to tens of millions of Turkish citizens and create a border-free zone all the way from Turkey's border with Iraq, Iran and Syria, should Turkey ever join the EU. In reality, Turkey was far from joining the EU and remains so. But instead, Britain has lost rapid, shared access to EU databases and other shared knowledge on international crime and cyber-security. What cooperation remains is pale by comparison.

"You talk a good line, for sure, but here is where you belong, false prophet," I hissed and turned away, leaning heavily on my shield. I could stand the sight of him no more.

[Canto 21 & 22] So we went on to the next bridge, talking about things I shall not relate here. When we reached the summit, we stopped to look down into the fifth trench of this Eighth Circle. It was a marvel of darkness. Below us, bubbled a dense black gunge of boiling pitch; the sort used to caulk wooden boats. I could see nothing in it, no tortured sinners. I gazed, mesmerized. Each bubble swelled and exploded. The ones in the middle left a gluey hollow, which re-filled almost imperceptibly before a new bubble formed. Near the side, each burst splashed across the banks in sticky smears. The soft plop, plop, was strangely soothing with a faint backing chorus of invisible laments.

"Watch out! Watch out!" cried Virgil and dragged me to his side. I turned to peep at what I really ought to have fled already. Horror! Right behind us was a dark demon-like figure, running around the ridge in our direction. Even from a distance I could read viciousness in his every move, ferocious, strong, but lithe and light of foot. Slung over one high sharp shoulder, he carried a sinner in a fireman's lift, with one hand gripping the ankles.

"Internet trolls," whispered Virgil. "Don't move a finger."

When the figure reached our bridge, he spoke: " 'ere you go, Junckjerker. Anuvver one for you! Plenty more where 'e came from in vat Westminster place. Watch how easy vey make a yes from a no, if yer give 'em enough cash."

He hurled the naked sinner down, turned and raced back down the flinty slope. No mastiff, unleashed after a thief, ever moved so fast. The sinner sank into the pitch and re-appeared, bottom up, smeared black. But more trolls, gathered under our bridge, invisible to us, shouted: "This is no place to show your Sacred Face. Ha ha, arse down, you! You're not here for a Sunday swim. If you don't want to feel our prongs – like this! – get back under."

They poked at him with long-handled, long-pronged forks – tridents, really – the way cooks push chunks of meat deep into the stewpot.

"Now tango in the dark!" they sang. "Pull what scams you can down there."

"Try to get out of sight," whispered Virgil to me. "Hunker down behind that rock spur, there, and wait till I signal. Best they don't see you yet. But don't worry. I know how to handle this lot. I've done it before."

I did as he said and watched him advance down the embankment, firmly and calmly. With all the tempestuous rage of a pack of hungry dogs spotting a lone wanderer, the trolls burst from under the bridge and rushed at him, brandishing their tridents. Virgil froze and stood his ground, his hands lifted in 'halt' in front of his chest.

"Don't even think of it!" he called. "First, let me speak to your leader and then decide if hooking me is right or wrong." It worked. They stopped and shifted from foot to foot, agitated.

"Go on, Junckjerker!" they shrieked. "That's you."

As their leader stepped forward, I heard one muttering, "What's he gonna get out of it?"

"So, Junckjerker, we meet again. You know I am immune to your tricks. Do you imagine I would be here again this time without some favouring aid of Fate or divine will? Let me and my companion pass. I have a duty to guide another through this savage place." The troll jerked his head in small movements from side to side, trying to spot this "companion", while not taking his eye off Virgil. Surprised by Virgil's confidence, he let his trident swing down to vertical, dangling by his side.

"OK," he told the others. "We let this one pass …. and his companion." The others looked restive, but not about to challenge their leader.

Virgil called up to me: "Come, Britannia. We may proceed."

I joined him quickly and stood glued to his side. All the trolls pressed forward, licking their lips, but I was not going to let them smell fear.

"Oh, tasty!" said one with unusually fleshy lips and hanging jowls. He brandished his trident. "Ripe for a poke in the backside."

"A deep poke! Get her in the notch, front and back," jeered others.

"Just cool it, XXPussyboss" ordered Junckjerker, swinging round to face them. "Cool it, all of yer." Then, turning back to us, he continued: "Further along this crag, you can't pass. The bridge is down. But if you go further around this cliff, arching round there," he pointed, "there's another outcrop that makes a path you can use. I'll send some of this team with you to watch for any sinner coming up for air. Go with them. They won't dare pull any stunts.

"So, forward, Playboy69! You too, @TheRealKGB, MakeAmericaGravyAgain,   HeadshotSniper666, BorrowMyJohnson, and Fartage. 060616, you're in charge. You'd better go too, NoBrentry, and you, XXPussyboss. Forward all!" I wasn't so happy about that last, as he grinned at me lasciviously.

"Search all around this pan for sinners, until you reach the unbroken spur. These two go unharmed!" XXPussyboss looked like he had other ideas.

"Virgil," I said. "If you know the way, let's go alone. I don't feel at all comfortable with this arrangement. Your eyes are usually so sharp. Just look how they scowl, grind their teeth and lick their lips."

"Don't worry," replied Virgil. "Their show is for the sad souls of corrupt politicians in this stew." My experience as a woman left me unconvinced, but I had to take Virgil's word for it.

The assigned trolls gathered together and poked their tongues out through clenched teeth at their leader. In response, he gave the order 'Quick march!' by firing out a loud fart. I have seen many brave knights strike camp, rally their troops and launch an attack to the sound of horns or drums. I have seen many a fleet set sail. Never any that set out to a fart!

Off we went, flanked by the trolls. Concentrated on the boiling pitch, I tried to identify sinners and avoid splashes as we moved. Every now and then, a sinner's back would emerge, arched, reminding me of nothing so much as a dolphin. Near the bank, I spotted a few snouts, like bull-frogs, their bulk below. Perhaps they felt the vibrations of our approach, for, quick as a flash, they dived below the bubbling gunge before the prongs could touch them. One was too slow and Headshotsniper666 speared his tar-caked side and flipped him onto the bank, where he flapped like a fish as he tried to dodge the trolls' fork jabs.

I had noted all their names, when they were first assigned. Now I listened to them squealing: "Get him, @The RealKGB! Fork his chest, 060616. Tear the leather off his ugly rump, Fartage."

"Can you manage to find out who that man is?" I asked Virgil.

Virgil stepped over authoritatively and asked the victim where he was born. The trolls fell back and paced menacing circles.

"Born London. Eton and Oxford (Brasenose)," came the reply. I recognized the polished voice immediately. The one who claimed to be a modern compassionate conservative, the 'hug-a-hoodie' type, the one who claimed he wanted to remain within a reformed European Union, but called a popular vote on such a complicated topic using a simple 'yes/no' question.

"And what has brought you here?" asked Virgil. I nodded to him vigorously. The trolls were restless. MakeAmericaGravyAgain, with jowls like a boar, was mock-lunging his trident in twist and rip motions. 060616 pinned his arms in a bear-hug from behind and called to Virgil to continue his conversation. If negligence were a vice, I would have answered for him. Insulated in his silk-lined, entitled world, he failed to grasp just how much and how many of the British people were hurting and struggling with problems aggravated by the policies of his own government and thus failed to make a sufficiently convincing argument for remaining.

"When I started as leader, I vowed to rid the party of corrupt MP's and establish new standards for public service," said the pitch-smeared victim. "But ten years later, after I resigned, they caught me with my hand in the cookie jar, you could say. I was only trying to do a pal a favour by using my old networks … and to save my shares."

"Surely you are not the only one? There must be others with you," said Virgil.

"Oh yes. We're quite a few."

"I've had enough of this," cried BorrowmyJohnson and skewered the victim's left arm, slicing out a prongful of muscle. Fartage was ogling his hams. But 060616 rounded on them with a filthy frown.

Our victim shook with pain and suppressed fear. He clutched his wounded arm. Nevertheless, he pressed on: "I can make others come. If the trolls stand back and promise not to attack, I'll sit here and whistle and they'll come. Now I'm here alone. Whistle and we're seven. That's our usual trick when the trolls are not around. They'll come. You'll see. And you will have sport."

"Nah, he plans to escape," said XXPussyboss.

"If he does that," I said, "I'll come after him myself. We'll hide here at the bridge and get all seven. Sport!"

The trolls giggled and, to my amazement, drew back

further to conceal themselves.

The victim gave two short whistles. Then he cried out: "They called me slippery and slippery I am." And launched himself into the pitch, diving deep.

The trolls shrieked with frustration. @TheRealKGB, the most humiliated, waded to his knees in the pitch, thrusting wildly with his fork. Four trolls, including 060616, ran along the bank, jabbing periodically in a vain attempt to spear the fugitive. Just beside us, furious XXPussyboss dropped his trident and flung himself at @TheRealKGB. "I told you, you idiot. Now we've lost 'em all." The impact brought them both down, wrestling in the shallows. But the bank fell steeply at that point and down they rolled into the boiling pitch. Two other trolls rushed to skewer them and drag them out.

"Now," whispered Virgil and grabbed my arm. I scooped up the fallen trident – it could be useful further on – and we ran together, like gazelles, up the bank. From the ridge, I risked a glance back. The two trolls who had fallen in had been pulled up on the shore by their mates. Too late. They were fried to a crisp. I dropped down the other side, out of sight.

[Canto 23] Alone now, we walked on in silence, Virgil leading, me behind. The scenes we had just witnessed kept somersaulting in my head, over and over. Then, in the way one thought so easily leads to the next, I saw Aesop's fable of the mouse, the frog and the hawk. 'Harm hatch, harm catch'. Those creatures had been so tricked, scorned and injured because of us, they were bound to be angry and more than likely they would come after us, like that pack of dogs we saw earlier. Goose bumps prickled down my back. I stopped and turned, scanning the route behind us.

"Virgil," I said, just as he halted. "I think we need to hide. Right now. That gang of trolls will be after us. I can feel they are not far behind. But I see from your face, you've already read my thoughts."

"I think we may be able to get down the bank into the next trench just up there on our right. If so, we should evade them."

And then I saw them, coming at us. Virgil snatched me up in his arms and, like a mother fleeing a burning house with her child, he launched himself down the steep and treacherous bank. With me bound tight to his breast, he slithered and leapt. As we touched down at the bottom, I looked back up. The vile creatures were ranged on the crest above us, snarling and swearing. To my enormous relief, assigned to guard Trench Five, it turned out they could not enter where we stood in Trench Six.

I turned my eyes back to our new surroundings. Ahead and behind us were people, moving very slowly along the trench. They wore hooded cloaks of a luminescent orange, so bright it dazzled me. With downcast eyes and the flashing, pointed hoods drawn right over their heads, their faces were invisible. But their heavy, shuffling gait betrayed their pain, as did their moans and the tears which fell to the ground in front of them. We stepped alongside. They moved with such difficulty that each swing of our hips brought us next to the one in front. I asked for Virgil's help to identify one who I might know, so I could learn more about their plight. Virgil stopped and turned to face the oncoming crowd.

"Try that one," he said, indicating one about three people back. It took a while for the figure to reach us. But, as he neared, I hailed him.

"Please, pause a moment," I said. I assumed it would cost him no effort, though I did wonder if he might have difficulty re-starting later. They seemed to need the momentum from each tiny step to make the next. "Tell me who you are and what punishment you are all enduring."

He did not – or could not – stop, but he lifted his head and searched my eyes.

"Welcome to the hypocrites' assembly," he said, still moving. I shuffled alongside. "These cloaks are thick with lead. And there ahead lies one on whom we must tread as we pass."

Indeed, a few metres ahead lay a man staked to the ground, his limbs writhing as each cloaked figure stepped on him and off the other side.

"Tell me his story?" I asked.

"In the past, he waved the flag for a form of conservatism that was pro-European, before Brexit had been conceived. But later he endorsed the Big Blond to lead them all. Some say he was just a hypocrite, hungry for power, who saw which way the tree was falling. Others say he was fooled into thinking that the Big Blond was really pro-Europe and letting the extreme anti-Europe thinkers believe otherwise as a tactical move; that, if the Big Blond were elected, he would revert. Anyway, this man was rewarded, after they won the election with an important role in justice. He was a lawyer, after all. There his hypocritical colours began to shine. He preached law abidance but, behind the scenes, he oversaw continued attrition of the legal system. He sanctioned the proroguing of Parliament, later declared illegal. He gave no negative advice when the Big Blond threatened to break the international treaty on special arrangements for Northern Ireland. He made no objection when his government ignored legal obligations on international aid. Worse, he publicly defended it as not so important, as long as the public did not make a fuss. Popularity was the only measure that counted. And then, once his professional credentials were beginning to look a little tarnished, he was dropped. No longer useful. Now he suffers here …. even more than the rest of us."

By then, we had reached the down-trodden sinner.

"Say something to him, Britannia," urged Virgil. What could I say? Such weakness evoked no sympathy in me. But his eyes swivelled and met mine, beseeching relief. I shook my head.

"You were part of an essential institution, charged with upholding the fundamental democratic principle of the rule of law to provide checks and balances on executive power. You abandoned your professional ethics when it suited your ambition. You are now where you belong."

I stepped over him and continued slowly, while the others punished him with their full weight.

Behind me, I heard Virgil asking first shuffling interlocutor: "Is there some exit from here to the right, so we don't need to call the internet trolls for guidance?"

"Oh yes," he said. "Sooner than you think, perhaps. Just ahead, there's a rock which juts out and vaults over all these Trenches, except it's broken here. You can clamber up the ruined side. The slope is gentle and the base piled high."

Virgil looked annoyed – with himself or another, I could not tell.

"So, the Chief Troll lied to us," he said.

"What do you expect, old man? Those internet trolls live by provocation and falsehood."

At that, Virgil waved and strode ahead, anger flitting across his face. I followed at his pace.

[Canto 24 & 25] I was dismayed by Virgil's distress. I had not seen him like this before. Was he feeling the pressure of what was to come? What did that mean for me? Were we running out of time against some deadline that he had not yet shared with me? I like to pace myself, when faced with a serious challenge. Greater transparency on what lay ahead would have helped me, instead of this slow, iterative reveal. But I could see this was not up for discussion. After all he had done for me, and no doubt still would, I could not risk pushing him too far. His hurt quickly disappeared. But I would bet he had simply suppressed it.

We walked on in silence and soon arrived at the ruined bridge. Virgil turned and faced me with that sweet, kind look I had first seen way back at the base of the mountain. He surveyed the landslip carefully and then traced the route we should take with an outstretched finger. After he had hauled me up behind him over an enormous boulder, he pointed to the next handhold and foothold in the rock ahead, while he gave me a leg up and shoved me from behind. This was clearly no way out for those with lead mantles. "Always first check if it can hold your weight," he said. I resisted the temptation to tell him that I was not a novice. I was relieved to see that our side of the trench was lower than the other, because all of this part of Hell tilts steadily down towards that central pit. Nevertheless, I was very out of breath. Virgil, of course, was weightless. Eventually we reached the point where a last building block had sheared away. I flopped to the ground, exhausted.

"Now you must shake off your indolence, Britannia," said Virgil. "No fame is won beneath the quilt or sunk in feather cushions. So, upward! On! Stop the panting! As you well know, in any battle, mind-power will prevail, unless the weight of body holds it down. Ahead is an even longer ladder that you must scale before your quest is finished. Come on now."

I heaved myself upright, controlling my breath to avoid his scorn. No-one calls Britannia weak!

"Let's go!" I said, "I'm ready for anything."

We ascended further and even steeper, up and along the cliff edge, carefully easing ourselves around rock spurs which blocked the path, bodies hugging the harsh stone. I kept up a conversation, so I would not seem feeble.

From the trench beyond, the seventh, I started to hear a voice, but I could make no sense if it. As we mounted the bridge, the voice was clear enough to recognize raging anger. I leant over, but the darkness down there was too thick. I could not see a thing.

"Virgil," I said. "Let's cross and then go down the far embankment a little way to get closer. From here I can't see or hear enough."

"Just do it!" he replied.

So, on the far side of the bridge, where it met the embankment again, I turned and descended halfway down into the eighth trench.

Merely thinking about what I saw there sends shivers down my spine: a brood of writhing reptiles of all different kinds. Among them, naked humans with skin of every hue on the planet ran in panic with nowhere to hide. Their hands were bound behind their backs by snakes, whose tails and heads ran between their legs and round their torso again to tie in knots behind. Just in front of us, a long, green serpent with bright red stripes along its back coiled and then launched itself at a pale man, running fast, and bit him exactly at the point where spine meets nape. He exploded into flame, a flash like a flare, and then disintegrated into a cascading shower of ash. Then, the dead dust gathered itself and transformed into the same man again. The sages say that a phoenix will die in its five hundredth year and then be re-born from the ashes of its own pyre. But its lifelong food is nurture drawn from balm and incense. By contrast, this sinner was struck down in pain and then rose again. Bewildered by the overwhelming shock of what just happened, he sighed and stared around.

Virgil asked him who he was. In a thick accent from east of the Danube came the response, at first hesitant and then finding its flow: "This place… I - I - am forced to answer you. I had some wealth and moved to London to buy my house in Mayfair and a hotel on Park Lane. It's easy to set up shop there. They ask no questions. In fact, my English friends tell me it's easier to set up a company than it is to get a passport. So much easier in England now than anywhere else. Good for business, eh? So, I gave a few millions to the politicians, I bought a football club and lived a nice life, a luxury life. But now, oh now, I face Eternity here." He started weeping.

"What made you so wealthy?" I asked. The weeping subsided. He raised his chin and snorted at me derisively, his lips curling. "You think I tell you that?"

From that point on, I understood the serpents were my friends. One entwined itself around his neck as if to say 'He'll speak no more'. A vivid black and yellow snake bound his arms and wound around his body so tight that he could not even make a fist. He fled; his legs still free.

Virgil was looking at me up and down in a curious way with a slight frown. Following his gaze, I looked down at my robe. It was covered in dark stains which gave off a foul odour of fish heads, mouldy onion, black, rotting potatoes and five-day old orange skins. My head spun.

"Dirty money, Britannia," he said and stepped forward with a rag from somewhere inside his robes and began to wipe me down. I felt more touched than ever by his care, but I knew I had been sullied deeper than my robe alone by this special form of theft.

"Who are you?" shouted a voice from below. While we were busy, at the bottom of the trench, three pale figures had approached. One turned to his mate and asked where another was. I could not catch the name. But as I watched, a huge black lizard, fully two metres long hurled itself at one of them. It clenched his belly with its hind claws and fastened to each arm with its front feet. Its teeth sank into his cheek. Then it slid one leg down his loins and shoved its tail between his legs and thrust upward, clenching fast between his buttocks. All its limbs were wound around him, like ivy barbed to a tree. It seemed the two of them were made of warm wax, as they began to melt into each other, their colours mingling in the way a flame licks across a page, creating ever-darkening tints, but not yet black, while the white dies.

The other two stood horror-struck, seemingly unaware that they themselves were merging into one being, melting together. From out of nowhere, a snake, peppercorn black, spurted across the road and struck this perverse, unified figure right in the middle, at the point where all of us receive our first nourishment even before our birth, and then it fell back at his feet, quite still. The pierced figure gazed at it and yawned, as if overwhelmed by sleep. He eyed the snake; the snake eyed him. Then, from his wound and the snake's mouth, smoke started to pour. The smoke streams met and began to intermingle. The two creatures began to react mutually. The snake's tail split into a fork, while the man's feet came together and his two thighs fused into one. I could no longer see that they had ever been separate. His arms began to retract into his armpits, while over there, the snake sprouted budding hands, like a tadpole. They swelled and lengthened in seconds and his rear end split to form two legs. Hide softened here and hardened over there. The fumes still hung around them in a gauze of strange colours, causing hair to sprout there and plucking the other sleek. Their gazes remained locked together. The one who had been a man fell flat, while the ex-snake stood. Upright now, he drew his eyes inwards. From the surplus pulp, two ears were formed and one glob slid down his face and gelled to form a nose. The lips plumped up.

The other, lying flat, pushed his nose forward. Then, like a snail pulling in its horns, his ears melted back, flush with his skull. His tongue, once whole, divided into two, while the other's fork closed right up. The man, transmogrified, hissed and wiggled off across the pit. The new man (previously a snake) spat on the spot he had left. He turned to the other man-lizard creature and they departed along the trench together, ignoring us completely.

From the shadows emerged a fourth figure, still man, skulking and looking carefully all around him. No doubt this was the one the three companions had been seeking, when we arrived. He had not spotted us, halfway up the bank.

"Who are you?" I asked. He started and crouched down into a ball. "We mean no harm", I added quickly to reassure him. "I merely want to know what brought you and those others here."

He lifted from his crouch, though suspicion and readiness for flight wafted still from every pore. I smiled encouragingly, as I began to recognize him.

"We are Captains of Industry," he said. "At least, we were. We owned and ran manufacturing businesses. We had created thousands of jobs in Britain, each one of us. We all campaigned for Leave. We all explained it would be good for our businesses and thus good for Britain. How it would free business up from unnecessary European regulation. We all voted to leave. Afterwards, when that pathetic deal – if you can call it that – was done, we saw we had to re-locate. Some of us moved most of our operations into Europe, because that's where our biggest markets were. Others, myself included, moved our operations to Asia."

"And what about the jobs? British jobs?" I asked.

"What do you mean? The jobs are where the operations are, of course. Labour's cheaper there too. Surely, I don't need to explain…. Next thing you'll be accusing me of Mansplaining you!"

"But you remained a British-registered company?" I interrupted.

"Yes, yes, of course. We all did. Why would that change? The corporation tax in Britain is very favourable and should get even better now we're out of the EU. What's more, I am British. And proud of it."

"And those who heard you on the Campaign trail and voted to Leave? Don't you think they expected more jobs in Britain?"

"I can't say what they expected. I am a business man, not a nanny – or a politician."

At this point, a gaggle of reptiles was approaching rapidly, blue and orange lizards, snakes in green, black and yellow. Our interlocutor dived for cover, though certainly in vain. I had no need to speak further and did not wish to attract the attention of the reptiles, so we turned and made our way back up the bank, Virgil pulling me from time to time.

[Canto 26 & 27] We continued on our lonely way through splintered rocks and outcrops, using our hands and feet where it was steep. For much of the journey I was preoccupied by what I had just witnessed, until we arrived at the middle of the bridge over the eighth trench. There below were individual flames, moving like fireflies in the dark. As they moved, they swallowed up human figures and created small columns of fire. I craned over the edge and peered below in an effort to make out who was suffering this fate. Had I not clutched a rock, I would have fallen for sure. The dancing flames in the dark made my head spin.

Watching my gaze, Virgil said, "Within the flames are spirits. Each wraps himself in what burns him."

"Yes, I had already gathered that," I said. "But I would like to know who is assigned to this dire punishment. There's one coming now, karate-chopping at the flames, but see how he has still just been enveloped."

"Keep your tongue in tight control. Leave me to speak. I know very well what you desire," he said and called down our enquiry to the flaming spirit below.

The flame first roared a while and writhed its pointed peak. It twisted and turned, first this way, then that, changing its form. Eventually, it spoke.

"As this flame, thus was I: hot and full of aggressive energy. In the beginning we said that, even with a Vote to Leave, we would not be leaving the Single Market. After the vote, we changed that. I said we would remain firm friends with shared values and shared prosperity, though we should enter the exit negotiations with economic and political self-confidence, because we were in a strong position. I didn't like the deal the Thin One negotiated. It was worse than staying in the EU."

"Ah," I nodded. I could not contain myself "Are you the one who voted for that deal on the third vote? And then, when it looked as though no deal would be possible, you argued that the original Referendum had given the mandate to leave without a deal, though that possibility was never raised beforehand?"

"I had a good brain. I was a good lawyer," he interrupted, glaring at me, as if poised to attack. "I argued well that the law did not require us to have a vote in Parliament to trigger the process for leaving under the

Maastricht Treaty. Let the judges who disagreed with me say what they like."

I watched a prominent vein throb in his temple, just below the receding hairline.

"Are you telling me that you abused your intellect to persuade others and suit your own ends?" I asked. "Is that not intellectual dishonesty? False counsel?"

"I was a model of self-discipline. But this thing it humiliated me," he lamented, suddenly sagging. It was as if naming his vice had punctured his bravado and thrown him back to where only burning self-pity remained.

"I had to admit, out loud, that I had under-estimated how much trade came through the Dover-Calais route," he said. "Perhaps I was a bit short on the homework, but others did much worse. Yet now I am punished without mercy."

The flame flickered low and continued on its way. Virgil and I continued too. We rounded the ridge and mounted the arch to cross the next trench.

[Canto 28] It is beyond mind or tongue to describe the full horrors of what we saw from the heights of the bridge over the ninth trench. Imagine all the wounded from every mediaeval battlefield all gathered in one place. And it was even worse! Close by, I saw a figure with dripping stumps at the end of his arms. He raised one to wipe his forehead and left it smeared filthy red with blood. Another hobbled by with his throat pierced through, his nose shorn off, one ear dangling loose, and his crimson wind-pipe open to the elements. I cannot continue. But closest to me was the worst. Split open from his chin to his crutch, his guts hung down between his legs. All his innards and heart were on show. My eyes fixed on him alone. And he gazed back, head tilted up to us. I recognized him. The enormous mouth, gaping open in a strangely rubbery face, which, in turn, seemed to be equal width with his neck. Always a showman, at that moment, he opened his chest still wider with his own hands and cried: "Look now, how wide I spread. They said I sowed division, discord and distrust, as did all the others here from throughout history. That is why we are all splintered and torn apart.

"Back behind us there stands a devil who decks us out this way very deftly with his sword. As we pass around this ditch, our wounds and gashes heal and we arrive back in front of him, whole, only to be cut into pieces all over again. But you, Britannia?"

He saw me start. "Yes, I know you. Of course, I do. What are you doing here?"

Before I could speak, Virgil replied.

"I am charged to bring Britannia safely through here. It is the first part of a long quest that lies ahead of her: a quest to recover her glory – some would even say, her balance – after the damage you and your like have done. On this journey, we pose the questions, you answer. Tell us what brought you here."

"Like I said earlier, they told me I sowed discord and whipped up fear. I merely pointed out that our women would no longer be safe if we allowed immigration to continue. You should thank me for that, Britannia. Millions of Romanians and Bulgarians were free to come to Britain. Imagine! And all those refugees from the Middle East and countries that treat women badly that the Germans encouraged us all to take. Worst of all, seventy-seven million Turkish just poised to come and seek their fortune and fill our doctors' waiting rooms."

"And have the numbers dropped? Or grown since that fateful day? Even by your own vile standards, you failed," I responded, surprised that I almost sneered with contempt.

"You can't be happy, Britannia, that there are parts of your country where you hardly heard English spoken. They were taking our jobs, using our services - which they didn't pay for, mind. I said we should put Britain first. Put you first, Britannia," he cried, pointing at me. In his state, the effort of talking was clearly taking its toll. He paused.

"Ah yes," I said. "It's so easy to whip up fear of The Other, isn't it? What did you think when white supremacists seized your messages and one shouted your 'Put Britain first' as he assassinated an elected representative of our democratic institutions? A woman, by the way."

"Well, of course, that wasn't what I intended. Dreadful thing! I think I am quite good at coining messages. But you can't hold me responsible for how they're used by some individuals. I had to stop the insidious creep of those Brussels bureaucrats, taking more and more decisions away from us. We had to take back our sovereignty."

That word again. The most abused word and undefined concept in this whole journey.

"And our common humanity?" I asked. "Universal Human Rights? Democracy? The values I have fought to defend so many times? Do you think stoking fear solves problems?" He ignored my questions and continued.

"I had to stop them. They were trying to create a political union by stealth. At first, they laughed at me. But not after the vote. Oh no! You should have seen their faces. Just wait and see how they'll all follow."

"And has that happened since? You are now where you belong!"

At this, he waved his arms and howled. From behind him, a headless torso approached, dangling his own head in his left hand, dripping crimson blood, and shoved our interlocutor forward to continue their circular march. I did not recognize either head or torso and soon lost sight of both spirits.

[Canto 29 & 30] My eyes had become drunk on this grizzly, mutilated crowd and would no longer move away. The adrenaline of the moment was spent and left a deep vacuum.

"Still staring at these miserable souls? Why do they plunge you so deep?" said Virgil. "You've not been affected like this in any of the other trenches. Are you trying to count them all? Well, think! This trench is twenty miles in circumference. We don't have time to stay longer. There is a lot more that you must see."

He turned and pressed ahead along our path. I followed in silence. What could I possibly do to heal the terrible wounds which this whole affair had inflicted? What could ever be sufficient? My own limbs felt like lead weights. For the first time, my helmet and shield – the symbols of my strength and standing – had become burdens I might not be able to continue to bear. Did the trident I had seized with such determination pose a threat to my power, rather than a clandestine boost?

I plodded on, dejected, until we found the jutting spur which indicated the tenth and final trench in this Circle. Even if I had not been able to see, I would have known I had arrived by the chorus of lamentations which floated upwards from the depths, barbed with pain and self-pity. I covered my ears with both hands. But I could not block my nose at the same time. I am not sure which was worse, the noise or the stench of rotting flesh.

Veering to the left, as we almost always did, we climbed the ridge and reached the highest point. From here, the power of Justice was crystal clear and the horrors with which fraud and falsification is punished. Across the dark floor of the pit, the guilty were clustered in stooks. Some sprawled across their neighbour's stomach, some across their shoulders. Others dragged themselves on all fours along the road – just for a change. None were able to lift their bodies higher. All were covered from head to toe in scabs and ulcers. Those sitting together scratched each other vigorously, fingers curled to give purchase to their nails. Blood and pus seeped from the festering sores, as slivers of skin, like fish scales, fell to the ground. But nothing they did seemed to relieve their itch. Without a word, we moved on step by step, overwhelmed by the sight, smell and woeful sounds of the sick.

I spotted one, sitting alone. Shunned or ignored by the

others, I could not tell. Beside him lay a long-handled, wooden back-scratcher, discarded. Instead, his right hand clutched a horse's currycomb and he raked in a frenzy at his prurient skin. Fine flakes, like frosty snow, showered from the comb and beads of red brightened in the furrows it left on his pallid shoulders, arms and thighs.

Following my gaze, Virgil called out: "You there, scratching until eternity, tell us who you are."

The incensed sufferer looked up at us, but never stopped his scraping.

"Who are you?" he called and winced with pain as a particularly deep scab flew from his inner thigh.

"I am here to guide this lady through the whole of Hell on her quest to restore her dignity and confront the beasts that have caused her harm," replied Virgil.

I added quickly: "May the thought of you never die in the memories of those living on in the new Britain. Tell me why you are here. I shall do no further harm to you than you already suffer."

"No-one could accept that deal the Thin One proposed. It would have left us worse off than were we never to leave the EU at all. Even the French would not have been idiotic enough to sign that deal! I stepped up to negotiate something better. I know how Brussels works. You have to take a hard line. It's the only thing they understand. I did it for you, Britannia."

"Ah, so you know me," I said. "From what you say and from the frosted flakes you peel from your body, I see you are the one they nick-named the No-Man. Tell me more."

"That's right. No fooling around with me. I never blink first and they knew it," he replied, puffing his barrel chest even as his finger nails tore at the pox all over it.

"But are you not the one who claimed you had negotiated a fantastic Withdrawal Agreement? The agreement that got rid of the controversial 'backstop' which kept Northern Ireland in the single market with all the accompanying standards and regulations and replaced it with a new 'Protocol'?"

"That's me!"

"But is that not the same Protocol that you now say has to be renegotiated in its entirety? You sold a dud!"

"No, no. Hold hard there. The problem is the pedantic way the EU interpreted it. They were nit-picking. And they insisted on the European Court of Justice being the final arbiter of disputes. That was an absolute red line! How could the court of one party be arbiter for both? It's a fundamental principle! Red line!"

"But was that not always their position? Had you not agreed that very point a year earlier without a fuss in the 'fantastic, oven-ready deal' you advised the Parliament to accept? Why was it not a red line then too?"

He scratched frantically from top to bottom and his limbs began to twitch.

"And was there not a subsequent trade agreement which had to be re-negotiated on fish and omitted trade in services altogether, including financial services? Even though service exports to the EU were huge and ran a surplus, compared to a deficit in manufacturing goods. I hear that service exports to the EU are falling fast now. How is that possible if it was such a good deal? You're a counterfeiter."

"It was just a negotiating tactic," he pleaded.

"Negotiating with whom? Europe or with British politicians and the electorate? Same as you advised signing a deal that neither you nor the leader had any intention of implementing."

"We could not let Brussels dictate rules and standards to us. We could not be a client state. I did it for you, Britannia. For your sovereignty."

"Sovereignty," I snorted. "How did your hard-line posture match up to the closed ranks of twenty-seven European countries standing in solidarity with each other? You ended up deliberately making demands you knew the EU would reject, so you could scapegoat them for your mistakes. You sold the voters a dud and then dug yourself into a self-defeating trench of absolutism on 'sovereignty'?"

"Long words, Ma'am! Long words!"

"Do you really feel no shame? Did you not see the piles of new red tape, while you claimed trade would be more open after Brexit?" I asked, searching for his shifting eyes.

"It's not my fault if the rest of the Cabinet did not take the opportunities that Brexit offered. I was not responsible for the slow action on reducing regulations and I was not responsible for taxes rising." His right-hand fingernails dug in hard to a spot just below his heart.

"What opportunities? You even hired an advisor <u>after</u> Brexit to start identifying the opportunities it offered. That tells me you did not know what they were."

"Well, of course, we knew. We just….." he stammered.

"Wasn't your whole career in this business a fraud? Had you not argued in a previous job that Brexit would bring serious economic risks? And did you not change your tune, when you saw the opportunity for a change of job with greater status? Adviser to the Big Blond whose political star was rising? And was it not you, who puffed yourself up to play at being a politician in government without facing an election? Did you not wangle a peerage as the alternative route? Please, correct me if I'm wrong."

I waited. He scratched and looked at the floor, mumbling.

"Your silence tells me you were serving yourself before you were serving me," I concluded. "Your rise was my fall. You are where you belong."

Suddenly, a pair of naked figures came into view, running fast. They gnashed and thrust like pigs released from their stye after months of confinement. One lunged at our interlocutor and sank its teeth into the nape of his neck. He howled as it dragged him, belly scraping, along the pit floor. I strained to see what had become of him, when I heard Virgil speak:

"Go on! Just hang around here watching!" I had never heard him use sarcasm before. He must be feeling the pressure. "It won't take much more before I shake you."

Indeed, that last angry sentence did shake me, though it was not exactly what he meant. I turned to him, my face red with shame, like a school-girl caught out dreaming in class. It had been a while since I had been reduced to that. As if I were indeed dreaming of some dreadful thing about to happen, I yearned, in the dream, for it to be a dream, so I desperately tried to say something to excuse myself, yet found myself unable to speak. And, by my very struggle, I actually did excuse myself, though I still thought I could not. Complicated, eh?

Virgil waved his hand and said, "Oh, don't worry. A far greater fault would be cleansed by the amount of shame you are displaying. So, come on. I will be by your side. Just don't waste any more time and remember that wanting to see someone suffer is a low desire."

5 THE DARKEST DEPTHS

[Canto 31] Thus, the same tongue that chastised me also soothed me - like Achilles' spear. We turned our backs on those dismal trenches and, in silence, mounted the bank which circled around. I could only just see in front of my feet. The light was dwindling: less than night and less than day. Suddenly, a high horn, louder than a thunder clap, shattered my reverie and echoed around us. I focused my eyes on the area which I thought must have been the source. As I watched, shapes started to emerge, like city towers.

"What town is this?" I asked Virgil.

"Now your brain is rushing ahead of what your eyes can see through these wreaths of shade and getting a blurred picture," he answered. Would I never get it right again? "Go closer and you will see clearer." Then with touching tenderness, he took my hand and added. "But first you should know that those are not towers of a city wall. They are giants. They are standing within the last and **Ninth Circle**, waist deep, around the rim."

As we moved closer, the darkness became less dense, like a thinning mist. But in the process my mistaken image was replaced by dread. Thank goodness there are no animals in nature like these giants – a horrible combination of brain, strength and ill-will. We approached the first. He bellowed at us and rattled the chains that bound him to the rock. I could not understand a word he said, but it was clear he was not welcoming us.

"Stick to blowing your horn to vent your rage!" shouted Virgil in response. Then turning to me, he explained: "That is Nimrod. Thanks to his vain efforts to build the Tower of Babel, the human race is condemned to speaking in different languages, at first incomprehensible to each other. And, no-one speaks his language. As you well know, the inability to communicate clearly with each other provides fertile breeding grounds for mistrust and fear. Leave him be. We must go on."

We continued until we reached a giant who was not restrained in chains.

"Antaeus will lift us down into the Ninth Circle," said Virgil, nodding a greeting to the gentle giant. "Since his defeat by Hercules, he will do us no harm, but he cannot leave this place."

The giant held out an enormous hand, the flesh cushioned like a bouncy castle. Gently, he scooped up both Virgil and me and closed his fingers around us to prevent us falling. His face – not unkind - loomed over me as we rose, swung and then swooshed down, down, bending low, until his fingers opened and he set us lightly on the ground in those terrible depths that swallowed Lucifer, the fallen angel, and Judas Iscariot and Brutus, the arch-traitors. Without delay, he swayed up again, straight like a ship's mast, and his face was lost to sight, though it lingers in my memory.

[*Canto 32*]   Nothing, but nothing, could have prepared me for what I encountered here in the **Ninth and Deepest Circle** of Hell. I am not sure that the words I have can adequately squeeze the juices of my memories about that malign and melancholy hole - the place where all the rocks above converge their weight. It is no joke to try and describe the bottom of the universe; no task for the faint-hearted. Those who dwell there would have been better off unborn.

From deep within that dark well at a point even lower than the giants' feet, I gazed up at the sheer black walls of rock. They seemed to go on forever. I could no longer see the sky. Slowly I turned through 360 degrees, trusting that Virgil and I would somehow emerge from this hole.

"Watch your step!" I heard a voice out of nowhere. "Be careful not to step on our heads."

Looking down, I saw we were standing on a lake of ice, clear as glass, frozen thicker than any lake I had ever seen. Fixed in this lead-blue prison, I saw human snouts just poking above the water line, like frogs in Spring when most of us are dreaming of the end of winter and the birth of new life. And further over were some heads above the water line, clenched at the point on their breast from where we begin to blush. Their teeth chattered rhythmically, like storks' beaks, bearing witness to the cold and their eyes to their pain and suffering. As I stared, I recalled more of Virgil's earlier words: 'The Ninth Circle is reserved for those who deceived people who trusted them and had cause to trust them....: the traitors, who betray special bonds. They have betrayed their family, their guests or colleagues, their own benefactors and/or their nation'.

Among them, I spotted a large head with tousled, pale blond hair and a beaky nose, which dripped. His red-rimmed, blue eyes seemed to retreat into his skull, though his pain shone out like a laser. I knew him immediately. No need to uncover the rest of his swollen, shambolic body. I slid my feet across the ice between the other heads to where he shivered. I could sense Virgil at my side, just behind my left shoulder.

"So here you are at last," I said, brightly. Meanwhile, I surreptitiously checked my grip on 'my' trident. Virgil had said at the start: 'You must confront the beasts that writhe in the depths.' It looked like the time had come. I knew that only the trolls' trident could do the job properly in this evil place.

"Oh wow! Britannia! What a surprise! I mean…. thank God, you've come. I.. I.. I didn't really expect you," he stuttered and then, recovering himself, "Great stuff, old girl. It's going to be a bit of a job to dig me out of this cold hole. But you're the one, the one who can do it. Fantastic to see you! You're looking well, may I say ….. unlike me, I guess."

"'Looking well', did you say? Do you know where we are?" I asked, frankly incredulous, though I knew I should not have been. "And do you know why you are here? If so, tell me."

"Well, I expect you know, old girl, that I used to be a bit of a lad. There are so many fine women out there with fantastic boo.. brains, doing fantastic jobs, changing the landscape of industry, wonderful entrepreneurs, the kind Britain needs. When you're an optimist like me, you sometimes get carried away with enthusiasm and one thing leads to another... well, you know."

"What about the lies? The lies to your wives and children?" I responded, gently.

"Lies? Well, perhaps in my enthusiasm I focused more on the good bits, on what they needed to know. There's no point in hurting people, if you don't need to. Now, if you could just…."

"Is that all?"

"Isn't it enough for now? I am ashamed of myself. The people of Britain expect me to be focused on the job, of levelling up across the country, bringing improvements in everyone's lives. They don't want any more distraction by my peccadilloes. I am totally repentant and you will all see that things are going to be different from here on. Now, can you just help dig me out of here and off we go to get started on a new chapter, suitably chastised and washed clean. I got Brexit done, remember?"

"Yes, I do remember," I replied. "And I have seen the consequences. Born of more of your lies, empty promises to flatter your ego, irresponsible statements that many voters, struggling to make ends meet, wanted so much to believe, while you party-ed with pole-dancers and quoted Churchill."

"Oh, come on, Britannia. You know as well as I do that it's a long-term project. We're going to have a fantastic Global Britain, great relations with our friends across the Channel and bold new deals with partners around the world. Britain will be the centre of the world again …."

"And you will be king, I suppose?" I snapped.

"Well, if that's what the great British people want…." He grinned.

Something in me snapped. I had rehearsed so many statements I wanted to make to whoever or whatever I would find down here – and I must admit, I had suspected he at least would be here – points about betrayal, not just of family, but also of colleagues and the whole nation. But I never got there.

"You are no leader. You are a shallow, self-absorbed, feel-good buffoon. You turned me into a laughing stock. You will stay here!" I cried and swung my trident up, twirled it in my hand like a cheerleader, and brought it down hard on his blond head. I shoved him down under the ice, drowning his yelp of pain. For a moment I saw his hands pressing up against the glass-clear ice beneath my feet. The shaft of the trident jerked and pulled in my hands. I gripped tighter and leant my whole weight on to it over the ice-hole. Images of the trolls, forcing the sinners into the boiling pitch flashed through my mind, alternating with images of battles I had fought and won earlier in history. Gradually, the jerking softened and then became still.

I sank back, sitting, spent, breathing heavily, my trident flat on the ice beside me. The other sinners' heads had retreated downwards, until nothing but a few raised pimples of a snout could be seen. No clattering stork-beaks of teeth could be heard. Silence! The black cliffs loomed over me. Was this it? Was this all? I turned my head to Virgil, who stood in silence behind me. Adrenaline seeped out of me. The cold seeped in.

"Now what?" I asked in a small voice. Could my teacher tell me that? Had I spoiled it all? Would I never be able to overcome my pride? After all I had been through, on this journey, and throughout history, was I doomed to act impetuously when angry and always when it was least needed? Virgil's sigh broke my self-absorption.

"This is not the end, Britannia. We have further to go," he said, quietly.

I am Britannia. I stood. I brushed the ice crystals off my outer robe and re-arranged it around my shoulders, where it had shifted in the struggle. I rolled my shivering shoulders and tried to square them firm, stood tall. Alongside Virgil, I moved forward into the dark, skating my shoes forward on the ice between the frost-bitten heads protruding still. Even today, I shiver still whenever I see a frozen puddle, remembering.

After a while of advancing, peering through the gloom, I spotted a larger lump. Approaching nearer, I saw it was two heads, frozen so close to each other that one head was almost on top of the other, like a hood. Nearer still, I saw the teeth of the upper head clench deep into the back of the lower one, where the brain meets the nape, in the way the starving devour bread. He ripped and chewed and then began to gnaw at the top of the skull, already daubed with dark red blood.

"You, who are you and why are you showing such bestial hatred to another human?" I called, in shock.

[Canto 33] Pausing in his savage meal, the sinner raised his mouth and wiped it clean on the few strands of hair left on the victim's large head. They were bright blond. Unmistakable!

"This man betrayed our cause. He was too weak to lead. He dithered and swayed in whichever direction the winds of popularity blew. I backed him at first and then I betrayed him, and now I am condemned to eat this vile, foul-tasting meal until eternity."

The slight whine in his voice and baby face were sufficient clues for me of his identity, though he had lost his trademark black-framed glasses. He had been wearing them, when I had seen him in an earlier Circle, walking backwards. The false prophet. I recalled how he had supported the Big Blond through the entire campaign to Leave. And then he had stabbed him in the back by announcing the day before the party leadership elections that he himself would stand for the reasons he had just repeated to me now.

"You knew how he was from the start," I responded. "The fault is as much yours for aiding his rise and for returning to his side after he beat you in the second leadership election. On top of betraying him as your colleague, together you and he betrayed the nation. You are strangers to Trust. You deserve each other."

Now I understood why he had fallen even further into this eternal pit. I continued:

"For you, ideology trumped everything. But you miscalculated and I, Britannia, am left to soldier on alone, weaker and poorer. Here is where you will be held accountable for the damage you have done. Enjoy your meal!"

He gave no answer. When I finished speaking, he gripped the skull again in his teeth, grinding as strong as a dog against the bone. We turned and moved on.

My stomach churned at what I had just witnessed. My own face had begun to freeze immobile from the chill, unable to show any emotion. Nevertheless, I could swear I felt a breeze against my skin.

"Where is this air current coming from?" I asked Virgil. "Surely, at this depth, nothing stirs. Are we getting close to a way out?"

"Come on! This way. Soon you'll see what causes this," he replied. His tone was not exactly reassuring. How much more of this was there to endure? He hastened on ahead. I followed.

[Canto 34]   Suddenly, he stopped. "Fix your eyes forward," he said. "Can you see it?"

Like a windmill seen from a distance in a thick fog or when darkness has just fallen, I could just make out some huge contraption moving. I shrank against the wind behind my guide. There was no other shelter at all. Here, the sinners were above the water-line, but completely encased in transparent ice, like gruesome paper-weights. Some lay flat; some were vertical; one with head high; another, soles aloft; and one bent like a bow, face to feet.

"Who are these?" I asked Virgil softly.

"They betrayed their benefactors," came the distracted answer and no more. He was pressing forward, though cautiously, his attention trained on that contraption in front of us. Before I could inquire further, the corner of my eye glimpsed a flash of pale yellow flitting across the gloom at head height behind some of the deep-frozen figures beside us. Senses alert, I snapped my head round to peer further and caught Virgil's sleeve. He halted and followed my gaze. There it was again. Virgil saw it too.

"Halt! Who goes there?" he cried, in a strange voice that was not loud enough to reach far or echo in this gloomy pit, but carried well in the direction it was focused to the side of our path.

From behind a particularly large ice block stepped the Big Blond, beaming and holding out his arms, he waddled towards us. He had put on even more weight. Imagine my amazement! What was happening here? My fingers tightened again around my trident. I had pushed him beneath the ice until he breathed no more. I had seen his head eaten – dead or alive, I didn't know and didn't dare to consider - by his poisonous, traitorous colleague. Now here he was, seemingly whole again.

"Welcome, Britannia, to the inner sanctum, the keep, of the City of Dis!" he said, his blue eyes dancing with glee.

This, from the same man who had been pleading with me to help him escape from this place. Or had I misunderstood? I was dumbstruck. All my senses began to work overtime, preparing for further surprises, but I could not speak. Even Virgil looked taken aback.

"I am so glad you made it to here," said the Big Blond.

'Something is very wrong', shrieked every fibre in my being as he approached, arms open wide towards me. No time to think. He surely intended to hug me. Danger! Danger! But my feet were rooted to the spot. Very quietly, I shifted the trident to horizontal, hiding most of it behind my back and keeping it close to my side, concealed by the folds of my outer robe. As his hands reached my shoulders, I struck hard, driving the three prongs forward and upward into his protruding belly. Pssssshhh! As if from a deflating tyre, a rush of foul-smelling air hit my face, forcing my eyes closed for an instant. I opened them just in time to see a fragment of the Big Blond spiral through the air, a burst balloon. In front of me, instead, stood the man I thought we had left in the first trench of the Eighth Circle above us – the Big Blond's pimp. He was doubled over, gasping for breath. My trident blow had knocked him back a few steps and clearly winded him, but no worse, I guessed.

A colourful fragment of the exploded balloon landed at my feet. I bent my knees, picked it up with my left hand and stowed it in my inner pocket. A rubbery souvenir. All the while, I kept my grip firm on my trident and my eyes focused on our host, if I dare call him that. Eventually, he stood.

"Pity about that costume. I was rather proud of it – or him. He always was a man of no substance, an empty shell. He lied so naturally, so blatantly. It was easy to imitate him and turn his weaknesses to our advantage. Nobody knew the difference. He – the real one - was so lazy and had such a poor grasp of detail, we needed to be able to double up from time to time."

I stood in shock. All I could stutter was: "Why? Why did

you do it? Did you really think Britain would be better off after Brexit, a better place? Look where it led you now?"

"Oh, Britannia! No-one knew if it would be good for Britain. Still, no-one does. And that includes me. But that's not really the point. The country needed disruption, sea change, renewal as a science- and technology-based economy: revolution. Get rid of out-of-date institutions and the Blob." His eyes widened fanatically. "There's something wrong with a political system that offers the electorate a choice for Prime Minister between two candidates as blatantly incompetent as we were offered last time."

"You have a point there," I said. "So it was you who set out to disrupt the checks and balances in our institutions, side-stepping Parliament, the illegal proroguing, rolling back judicial oversight, starving the courts of resources and more? Reform is necessary, I agree, but not concentration of power in the hands of the executive."

I never heard his response. At that moment, a roar echoed down the ravine from the direction of the contraption.

"He needs more food," said our interlocutor, his head snapping towards the sound. He turned from us and hastened down the passage.

Virgil beckoned to me and we followed, more cautiously.

"Now see!" urged Virgil. "This is where you must muster all your strength." Now I saw that the Thing I had glimpsed from afar, that created this breeze, was no contraption. It was alive.

Just ahead of us I saw that creature which had once been fair, but had fallen from the heavens to this great depth, where he ruled supreme. My mouth went dry, my limbs felt weak, my heart started beating wildly. I simply cannot describe the sensations that coursed through my body and mind. I neither died nor stayed fully alive. The giant emperor of this realm of Grief and Gloom bulged from the ice from his breast up. If once he was as lovely as now he was vile, then truly all Grief must flow from him. His enormous head carried three faces. The forward-facing one was bright vermillion. Joined to it, roughly above the mid-point of each shoulder, were two others. One was whitish yellow, the other pale brown. All three faces met on the crown of his head. Two wings spread from under each face's chin, strong and immense, larger than any sail I had ever seen. They were bat-like, not feathered, and produced the wind of which I had felt the edges earlier. But here it blew much colder - cold enough to freeze the Cocytus River beneath our feet. All six of his eyes were weeping. The tears ran down his cheeks and mixed with the bloody foam that oozed from his jaws. Two of his mouths held sinners, raked by his teeth, in agony. For the one gripped in the front-facing mouth, the teeth were nothing like as vicious as the claws, which sliced and tore the skin on his protruding back. His head was locked inside, his legs flailed.

"That soul, who suffers the most, is Judas Escariot," said Virgil. "The other on the left with his head hanging out is Brutus. Look how he writhes without saying a word." The jaws of the right face were empty.

Keeping ourselves just out of sight, we watched. Now it was clear that the man we had just 'uncovered' was Satan's Pet. He stood facing the Lord of Hell, tiny and vulnerable, but seemingly not in danger. Lucifer bent his head to him and they appeared to communicate, while the three-faced monster continued chewing. Then Satan's Pet turned and loped off into the shadows. Within moments, he returned, dragging someone behind him. It was the same man I had left a long way above in the Sixth Circle, surprised and offended that I would not help him from his scorching tomb back there.

He still had his round wire-framed glasses. But his long thin face looked a little harder than when I had last seen him and his black and silver hair was less neatly combed and parted.

"Britannia," he called. "Such a joy to see you again," his

voice heavy with sarcasm. Satan's Pet allowed him to halt.

"I have learned many things on this journey," I responded. "I was fooled by your boyish demeanour and I under-estimated you. I shall not make the same mistake again. I have a question for you. Tell me, who benefits from your holy grail of low-tax, low-regulation, so-called 'entrepreneurial' economy?"

"The ones who always have, of course," he drawled, without hesitation. "That's what we were bred to do. That's how it was in your glory days and that's what we will have again."

I raised my eyebrows. "You are making Britain the 'go-to' destination for money-launderers, thieves and financiers of terrorism, while honest, hard-working people are squeezed beyond their limits and left to compete against unbridled power? Is tolerance of fraud now part of the economic strategy?"

He sneered at me. "Oh, come on, Britannia! You don't really care about the Little People, do you? You never used to, back in the old days."

"You mean back in the nineteenth century," I replied. "Have we not learned the lessons from leaving raw capitalism unleashed, free from scrutiny? Have we not advanced? Do we not know now how to harness its power and to apply ethics and regulation to curb and protect ourselves from its worst excesses? Times have changed."

"Less than you think," he retorted. "Don't be so naïve. Don't tell me you're going 'woke'. Britain is a nation of rulers and ruled. It always has been; it always will be."

"Your contempt for others less fortunate than yourself disgusts me," I said. "And you claim you did it for me! Bah! You sold a false vision and betrayed the electorate you were chosen to serve. You betrayed me! Having put major blockages in the path of the previously thriving trade in manufactured goods and legitimate services with our largest trading partner, you want to make up the economic shortfall by turning me into a global whore. Wealth for whom?"

He sneered again, waving a dismissive hand. "Let others look after themselves. Besides, you don't make the poor rich by making the rich poor."

"Now I know why you have been brought down here," I said. But my words were lost in another roar from Lucifer. Satan's Pet grabbed the man by his greasy hair and dragged him to his fate. What struck me most in the ensuing minutes was that he seemed to be accustomed to corporal punishment, as if it were normal and to be endured.

"Come," said Virgil. "It is time for us to depart this hole. You have seen it all."

At his request, I put my arms around him, the same way I had done before. And as he took up my weight, my body hung, exhausted, in his grasp. Only my hands clung firm to my wrists around his neck and my legs curled around him. How he carried me so effortlessly, I shall never know. It is a secret of the dead. He waited for his moment, and when the monster's wings were fully open, he lunged forward and grabbed a handhold in the furry sides. Fist over fist he took us down between the matted pelt and crusts of ice. When we reached the hip joint, where the haunches are at their thickest, with enormous stress and strain, Virgil pivoted to bring his head to where his legs had been. From there, he clutched and grappled with the fur as if he were climbing, while I was thinking: 'We're heading back down, deeper into Hell.' Between his puffing and heaving, he said: "Cling tight. It is via stairs like these that we must escape all this evil."

We emerged through a fissure in the rock and he perched me on the rim, while he carefully followed. We were in a coarse-stoned natural cave. There was light: weak, but nevertheless light. I lifted my eyes, expecting to see Lucifer as I had left him. Instead, I saw his shape inverted, legs upward.

"On your feet," ordered Virgil. "We must move on."

"Before I tear my roots from this abyss," I asked, "please explain, sir, why Lucifer is upside down and where the ice has gone? I am totally confused."

"You imagine you are on still the other side, where I grappled the fur of the evil one who pierces the world. But when I pivoted, we crossed into the upper hemisphere and you now see Hell as it really is," he replied. "Come now! Take a deep breath and gather yourself. We are out of Hell, but our road through Purgatory is long and hard. Remember, there is no other way for you. We have no time to waste."

I heard water falling in a rivulet. Navigating by sound, we arrived at an opening in the rock, eroded over the ages, totally camouflaged, but wide enough for us. Without hesitation, we took the hidden path once more towards a shining world. We climbed, Virgil first, me following as before until a tiny aperture appeared and grew as we climbed. Sky! We emerged under a dark blue night sky with a circle of bright yellow stars.

END

DIAGRAM OF DANTE'S INFERNO

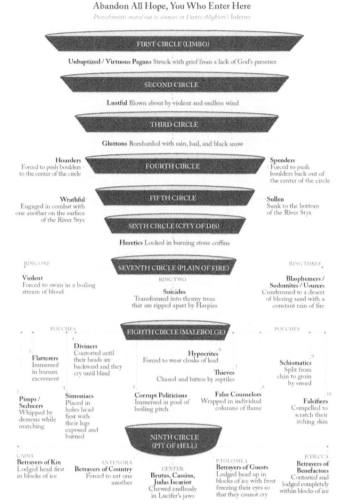

Abandon All Hope, You Who Enter Here

Punishments meted out to sinners in Dante Alighieri's Inferno

FIRST CIRCLE (LIMBO)

Unbaptized / Virtuous Pagans Struck with grief from a lack of God's presence

SECOND CIRCLE

Lustful Blown about by violent and endless wind

THIRD CIRCLE

Gluttons Bombarded with rain, hail, and black snow

Hoarders
Forced to push boulders
to the center of the circle

FOURTH CIRCLE

Spenders
Forced to push
boulders back out of
the center of the circle

Wrathful
Engaged in combat with
one another on the surface
of the River Styx

FIFTH CIRCLE

Sullen
Sunk to the bottom
of the River Styx

SIXTH CIRCLE (CITY OF DIS)

Heretics Locked in burning stone coffins

RING ONE

SEVENTH CIRCLE (PLAIN OF FIRE)

RING THREE

Violent
Forced to swim in a boiling
stream of blood

RING TWO

Suicides
Transformed into thorny trees
that are ripped apart by Harpies

**Blasphemers /
Sodomites / Usurers**
Condemned to a desert
of blazing sand with a
constant rain of fire

POUCHES

EIGHTH CIRCLE (MALEBOLGE)

POUCHES

Diviners
Contorted until
their heads are
backward and they
cry until blind

Flatterers
Immersed
in human
excrement

Hypocrites
Forced to wear cloaks of lead

Thieves
Chased and bitten by reptiles

Schismatics
Split from
chin to groin
by sword

**Pimps /
Seducers**
Whipped by
demons while
marching

Simoniacs
Placed in
holes head
first with
their legs
exposed and
burned

Corrupt Politicians
Immersed in pool of
boiling pitch

False Counselors
Wrapped in individual
columns of flame

Falsifiers
Compelled to
scratch their
itching skin

**NINTH CIRCLE
(PIT OF HELL)**

CAINA

Betrayers of Kin
Lodged head first
in blocks of ice

ANTENORA

Betrayers of Country
Forced to eat one
another

CENTER
**Brutus, Cassius,
Judas Iscariot**
Chewed endlessly
in Lucifer's jaws

PTOLOMEA

Betrayers of Guests
Lodged head up in
blocks of ice with frost
freezing their eyes so
that they cannot cry

JUDECCA

**Betrayers of
Benefactors**
Contorted and
lodged completely
within blocks of ice

Reprinted from *Lapham's Quarterly,* "Crime and Punishment,"
Vol. 2, No. 2 (Spring 2009), https://www.laphamsquarterly.org/